Crossroads

Crossroads

By Shaila

authorHOUSE®

AuthorHouse™
1663 Liberty Drive
Bloomington, IN 47403
www.authorhouse.com
Phone: 1-800-839-8640

First published by AuthorHouse   10/07/2011

ISBN: 978-1-4567-9610-5 (sc)
ISBN: 978-1-4567-9611-2 (ebk)

Printed in the United States of America

Dedicated to the handful of people in my life who truly bring out the best in me and wish the world for me

Foreword

You often wonder what influences you to be how you are, and who you are; what experiences shape you and mould you, to become the person you turn out to be. These experiences either influence you when you are growing up, or often while you *are* all grown up, to change you from who you used to be. This book is based on such experiences that influenced me as a child, as a teenager or as an adult; either my own or of those around me.

I have obviously thought about these experiences often—why it happened, what positive impact it had, what negative influence it had, and whether or not it could or should have been avoided. Sometimes these are within your control, but most often than not these are the outcomes of those around you, of those whose actions you cannot control or do not know how to. I have had so many of these experiences that made me think 'why me' or 'when is it going to get better'. I have heard in the media of celebrities who have been through such experiences. I know of friends who have been in similar situations as myself. Unfortunately, when I tried to assist and offer my support to guide them in the right direction, I was shot down. I realised no matter what the circumstances, eventually you just

Shaila

have to take matters into your own hands, and shape your own destiny. That's what I did, or at least tried to do. For me.

I used to be full of life, an extrovert, an open book. Being suppressed for years left me an introvert, closed off within myself, walking in the clouds lost in my own thoughts. Once in a blue moon I would come across someone who would make me want to open up and be the person I once was, the one that I truly admired, but the one I thought I had lost forever. Once in a while I would want to be that person again to someone who would make me feel I could trust them enough with my thoughts, and without any judgement. But soon I would realise I came across more neurotic than I would have hoped for, for I have lost all ability to express myself with comfort or confidence or without sarcasm in my voice. I have become distant even from myself, and distant from all that's considered normal in humanity.

Chapter 1

All set ready to go on a whirlwind trip around the world. Had my flights booked and itinerary confirmed—Asia, Europe and North America. New Year's Eve at the foot of the Eiffel Tower. Glimmering lights, fireworks, and thousands and thousands of smiling faces counting down to the New Year. Took a semester off university too so I could spend a remarkable eight-months trotting around the globe. Inexplicably excited.

A couple of months before my grand departure, I received a phone call from one of my girlfriends who I only hear from once in a blue moon.

"Teressa, so nice to hear from you! How have you been?" I ask excitedly. "How long has it been since I have spoken to you last?"

"Obviously too long, sweetheart," she responded cheekily. "What have you been up to?"

"Well, I am so glad you called. I am actually planning on going overseas in just over two months. I have this whole trip planned to the bone. I was going to call you before I left and invite you to a mini farewell I was thinking of having."

"Well, why wait that long? The reason I am calling is because I wanted to invite you to my birthday party next Saturday. I was really hoping you would be able to make it. We just haven't seen each other in so long!"

"Oh! I would love to but I am supposed to be working that Saturday. Let me check with work to see if I can swap my shift with someone else. I will definitely let you know within the next couple of days. Is that OK?"

"OK. Don't keep me waiting. Make sure you let me know soon, and better even, make sure you *can* make it," she emphasized.

"Alright. Talk soon." I replied before hanging up.

As it turned out, swapping my shift with someone on a Saturday evening was harder than I thought. So I had to call her back to let her know that unfortunately I would not be able to make it to her birthday extravaganza. She was, however, very insistent that I go over to her house the next day to have some of the birthday cake. I could not refuse.

I went over to Teressa's house the following Sunday. I had been working both the night before and on the day itself, so by the time I finally made it to her house, I was exhausted beyond belief. I could barely drive given how tired I was feeling, and it didn't help that she lived almost over an hour away from the city

2

centre. I lived in the opposite direction to her from the centre, but only about fifteen minutes away.

I did not stay long. I was looking forward to going home to get some much needed rest. I was working at a cafeteria at the time to pay my way through university. It was a part time job, but between studies and work, it meant I hardly found any time for myself. Meeting friends who lived any further than within a ten-kilometre-radius of the city centre was a rarity. I only had the luxury of meeting with them if they were around in the city for the day or I had been told weeks in advance to keep a day free. It was not something I enjoyed—having such a hectic lifestyle at such young an age, but it was about survival. I needed money to pay for rent, bills, food. I needed to maintain focus so my studies did not suffer while I spent too many hours working or socialising. How to lead a well-balanced lifestyle was something I had to train myself to do early on so as not to go insane from juggling all the many different things I had to fit in a day.

As I was leaving Teressa's house, I bumped into someone. He was waiting to come in as I was walking out the door. Tall, dark and handsome, some might say. If the circumstances were different, he would have caught my eye. At that stage though, in that moment, I was only focused on my upcoming adventure which I had spent so many months planning. I was definitely not keen on meeting any handsome strangers. Even so, someone inside my head suggested I should stay away from him. I was not sure what the random fleeting thought meant. I ignored it. I gave him a very quick glance while he walked past me at the doorway, as he tried to hold my gaze. I left after saying a quick 'hello', without waiting to be properly introduced.

A few weeks later, I received another surprise phone call from Teressa. She informed me that she would be in the neighbourhood on the following Tuesday, and would like to catch up for a movie. Tuesdays were the 'cheap' movie day of the week, and a very popular day amongst students to head to the cinemas. After working out all the details over the phone I decided to meet her Tuesday evening. My class would finish at six in the evening, and the movie she suggested we watch started at seven. So I planned to go and meet her straight after university. The ride to the cinema would only be ten minutes. Add to that the time it would take me to park the car and find her at the cinema, it would just give me enough time to meet up with her fifteen minutes before the movie started.

On Tuesday evening, there was a big surprise waiting for me at the movies. Not only did Teressa forget to mention that she would be bringing her boyfriend along, she deliberately also forgot to mention that the handsome stranger from the other night would be accompanying us as well. Here I was foolishly thinking that I was going on a girls' night out to the movies, but now it seemed more and more like a convenient set-up. This time around, we were properly introduced. He was Teressa's childhood friend. They practically grew up together, went to the same schools and had the same circle of friends.

Funnily enough, I can't even remember what movie we watched that night. I found him a very interesting person to talk to. We spent the entire time whispering to each other during the movie. How could we have so much to talk about? There was an instant undeniable connection. It was easy and uncomplicated. It lacked any pretence or vagueness. It was intriguing. At one point I did feel a little guilty for inconveniencing those sitting in the theatre around us. I usually never talk during a movie. Except on that occasion . . .

All I remembered was that the more we talked, the more we found things in common: both born in Australia with parents from Bangladesh. Both born in the same year. Both went back to Bangladesh at an early age, lived there until fifteen and then made the choice to start a new life back in Australia. Both of us returned to Australia in the same year, but to different cities. Finally, here we were, in the same city, at the same time, introduced through a mutual friend, getting along like a house on fire. The fairy tales you read during your childhood would have your head geared to believe that this was fate, it was 'meant to be': your own fairy tale in the making.

As we continued to whisper in the darkness of the theatre, completely oblivious to the movie or those around us, I felt something. He was sitting to my left, edging closer and closer so we could hear each other. At one point he leaned across towards my seat, with his right arm resting firmly on the arm-rest of his seat. For a brief moment his bicep brushed against mine.

There was electricity. I got a taste of what it meant to feel a spark, literally.

We swapped numbers after the movie. Well, rather, he gave me his—he already cunningly had mine. My dear friend decided to make sure he had my number without even asking for my permission. However, I didn't care about it so much now that I had spent two wonderful hours with him. As we were saying our goodbyes he asked me out on a proper date without hesitation. I was so impressed by his confidence that my heart wanted to say 'yes', but my head was saying 'no'. After pondering over it for a few seconds, I eventually let my heart trump my head. In keeping with the courageous journey I was about to set upon, I said 'yes'.

I drove home that night with a smile on my face. I reached home pretty late—it would have been well past midnight. As soon as I entered through the door, my phone rang, and guess who it was on the other end? We started to talk again. The conversation ended up being quite deep and meaningful, lasting more than half the night—about morals and values, about what we wanted out of life, about being brought up in a developing country like Bangladesh but trying to fit in as a teenager in Australia. About the struggles of teen life and having to cope with conflicting cultures. About the lack of sense of identity, and the constant search for it.

It was not easy for me to fit into the culture and lifestyle, into school and the social scene when I first returned to Melbourne. It was really difficult trying to find a balance between what I was taught of how to live a life of virtue while growing up and the predicament of teenage life in Melbourne. I loved my school, loved where I lived, but even so there was a constant battle in my head around all the social aspects. Where should or shouldn't I go, who I should or shouldn't mingle with, what should or shouldn't I do. Alcohol, smoke, or sometimes even drugs, seemed to be the normal way for the majority of the kids to live up their high school days. House parties were the norm. Even the so-called 'goody two shoes' would drink at a bare minimum—that was just how you socialised. If you wanted to fit in, you needed to participate. Or you could spend your weekends stuck at home on your own. That was never an attractive proposition to an ordinary teenager.

I was brought up differently to that, where drinking copious amounts of alcohol was definitely frowned upon. It was not as if I was very religious, or my friends and network for that matter, but I did grow up in a pre-dominantly Muslim society. My grand-parents were quite religious. My father—I did not remember seeing him pray at home, but that was because he was a tad lazy in nature. He did, however, enjoy discussing religion with us, as much as he did politics and history. My mother—she became more religious later on in life, mostly because of what life threw at her. I remember though that we were always told how a good Bangladeshi girl should behave. It was unimaginable for my parents to think any of their children would drink, smoke, go to parties and clubs or anything of the like. They would have been immensely shocked if they found out that even some of our friends in Bangladesh used to throw wicked house parties. May be that was the result of going to an English-medium school where a lot of the kids had lived abroad, saw what it was like elsewhere and tried to imitate the same when they returned to Bangladesh. Or maybe it was because they were influenced by the books available at the school library by various English authors or the shows they watched on satellite television. Some of the kids' parents knew, the ones that were more liberal, but not most. And definitely not mine.

Strangely enough though, I never participated in anything that may have had my parents disappointed in me. Even at these so-called house parties I wouldn't drink and definitely not do drugs—sometimes I was too naïve to even realise they had them around. I was always the girl that would mingle, socialise and have a good time, but without any enhancers, alcoholic or otherwise. I wasn't so because my parents were conservative and may find out. I just didn't want to disappoint anyone. It was more due to the fact that I was the middle-child and growing up believed I was less loved than the younger sibling and less respected than the older. So it was always about making sure I strived to achieve what my parents would expect of me. Trying to feel they were as proud of me as they were of my other siblings.

Even though my parents were strict in terms of their teachings or ideology, they were a lot more 'relaxed' than you would expect from a close-knit family in a third-world country like Bangladesh. The streets were not the safest to travel on, and poverty was rife. There were constant strikes, protests and demonstrations where small explosives sounding like firecrackers would go off every few hours. There were muggers on street corners and hijackers targeting the vulnerable on rickshaws. We were not, however, caged like a lot of teenagers our age would have been. We were allowed to go out on our own when we chose to. We didn't need to be chaperoned around—we could travel to and from school on our own, go over to a friend's place on our own and not necessarily have a strangely early curfew imposed upon us. Most of my friends on the other hand, and most definitely the girls, had chauffeurs driving them around or at the least had the house-maid chaperon them. Curfews were a normal way of teen life.

On that basis I must say I was quite lucky. Quite lucky to have more independence and freedom than others in my position, being able to do things my way. May be that's why as a teenager I also did not feel the need to rebel, but to do right by them. In Australia, there were more opportunities to readily get involved in activities that would not be considered appropriate by my parents, than in Bangladesh. Hence the constant battle in my head of what I should or shouldn't do. Where I should or shouldn't go. Who I should or shouldn't be with. Especially when I returned to Melbourne at the age of fifteen—I didn't want my mother to have to deal with anything other than just taking care of her children and putting food on the table. She had lost the most important person in her life less than a year ago, and didn't need any additional burden. Besides, I liked to believe that he was watching down on us from heaven. It made it easier to deal with the pain when things didn't go our way or when I was working too hard to make ends meet. Yes, the reason I had to convince my mother to move back to Australia when life got harder and harder in Bangladesh: *I had just lost my dad.*

Chapter 2

*I*t was a lovely Monday afternoon in the spring of 1997. The birds were chirping, the flowers were blooming, the sky—a perfect shade of blue. The smell of rain had passed and the breeze was slightly warm. The bell rang for the last period in school and all the kids filed out of the classrooms into the courtyard outside. Some of them changed out of their school uniforms and into their track-suits or shorts before running out to the courtyard, to get ready for the after-hours extra-curricular activities. The outdoor basketball court and the soccer field filled up quickly with those training for upcoming events. For others, there was a mad rush to get home. Some lined up to get onto the school bus that would drop them on the other side of town. Some had their chauffeurs waiting to take them home, while others had their house-maids waiting to guide them back on rickshaws. I, on the other hand, had neither. I was very used to just hailing a rickshaw from outside the school yard, negotiating a price with the puller for the ride and being on my merry way home. Most days I would meet up with my older sister to get home given we both went to the same school. But on this particular day, she decided to stay back and work on some assignments at the school library after-hours.

I hailed myself a rickshaw. As I was sitting there tightly holding onto the side with one hand and clutching my backpack with the other, listening to the rickshaw-puller whistle away, I looked around the neighbourhood in quiet contentment. *"Such a beautiful day!"* I thought to myself, *"It couldn't be more perfect!"*

As the rickshaw pulled into our drive-way I was surprised to notice tens of cars lined up across the road from it. *Probably one of the neighbours is throwing a party tonight and the guests are starting to arrive,* I mused.

I gave the rickshaw-puller what I owed and walked across to the main entrance. When I got closer to the front-door I heard voices coming from inside the house. It was unusual there to be people at our house at this time of the day. Dad would have still been away and mum would have been by herself. She was a house-wife.

Ah-huh, so maybe we are the ones with the guests. Yay! This day is turning out to be even better than I expected! Fourteen-year-old me got excited at the prospect of being surrounded by guests and not having to do any homework that evening.

I cautiously turned the key and pushed the door open while holding onto the door-knob. I could see many faces inside as the door became ajar, but none familiar. I stared confusingly at all the unfamiliar faces around me and ran inside to locate my mum. I ran towards her bedroom. The mood around me was quite sombre. I didn't know what was going on, but I was determined to find out. No one seemed to want to tell me though. They were acting like I was a little child who needed to be protected.

I ran up the stairs, glaring at the unfamiliar faces and halted as I approached my parents' bedroom. Finally there were some familiar faces around—my aunts, my uncles, my cousins, my nieces, and nephews. Random questions began to float through my mind. What were they all doing here? How come I wasn't told that they were coming over? Did my parents think I would have just left school early and not bothered with the rest of my classes? What was this all about?

I still couldn't see my mum, but an aunt came forward to greet me. She gave me a carefully-mastered smile and asked, "How was your day?"

"Pretty good. What's going on? What are you all doing here?" I countered in a chirpy voice.

"Come here and take a sit. I want to have a chat to you," came her response.

"Where is Ammu?" I probed. "I want to talk to her."

"Your mum is right here. You can talk to her in a minute. Let me have a chat to you first."

"No I want to talk to her first." I said in a determined voice. As I swivelled around, I saw her sitting right

13

in the middle of the bed with her feet firmly on the floor and her head down. She had a veil covering her forehead and her eyes were hidden underneath the shadow it casted over her face. I had not seen her wear a veil like that ever before, unless of course it was because she was doing her prayers. I called out to her in order to catch her attention, but she sat there silently, still. For a split second I thought I heard sobbing coming from that direction, but I couldn't be sure. I was ushered out of the room by my aunt.

"Here, take a sit." She pulled up a chair in our little study room, next to my desk.

I politely sat down, looking up at her with confusion in my eyes. I just wanted someone to explain to me what on earth was happening here.

"I am not exactly sure how else to say this to you, but your father has just passed on. I am so sorry!" my aunt said in a steady, calm tone of voice with a hint of sadness. She wrapped her arms around me to hug me tight.

My immediate reaction was to laugh out loud but I composed myself. *"It was all a joke; they were all trying to play a prank on me!"* I thought, almost sure of myself.

I had just seen a healthy, perfectly fit fifty-year old man walk out the door the previous morning, with a briefcase in one hand and a duffle bag on the other. He was heading out of the house to go to work that day as every other weekday, except that at the end of the work-day he was going to join some colleagues on a business trip some few hundred miles away; but he was due back home at the end of the week. He was going out of the city to the smaller towns surrounding Dhaka to meet with potential vendors, partners and what not—I was only fourteen and didn't understand the details or the significance of it all. All I knew was that it was something he had to do and his company wanted him to be the one making all the presentations in front of large crowds for something big that was about to happen.

My father was working in the public sector. He was a highly-educated man having done his PhD in Chemistry from the University of Melbourne, and was an ocean of knowledge. He was brilliant, hard-working and honest. Too honest. For someone working in the public sector in a country like Bangladesh with a moral compass, it was a hard life. With all his knowledge and credentials, he barely made enough money to support his family. He wasn't the one to take bribes or participate in the realm of corruption that engulfed the entire system. He refused to do so, ever. He was up for promotion multiple times, he was promised a raise every few years for all the hard work he put in, to be able to better support his family, give his girls a life he never had. But every time, every single time, it would not work out in his favour. The decision not to promote him, but rather a different colleague of his, would always come when he would have turned down an offer to participate in something shabby as proposed to him by his superiors. Year after year he kept doing what he was doing, with the promise of something better to come soon, but soon after he would have been disappointed. I had never asked him if he liked what he did, if he really enjoyed his work, and why did he still stay on for so many years. I supposed the answer would have been either the fact that the unemployment rate in the country was extremely high, or that he was just a loyal human being. Both were true, but I knew in this instance the latter was more likely to be the reason for his continuous devotion to an organisation that finally led to his demise.

As I sat there on the chair in my study-room trying to fathom what I had just been told, the events of the morning before flashed right before my eyes. To this day, I remember that morning as vividly as if it were yesterday.

I was getting ready that morning to go to school as I caught a glimpse of my father sitting at the dining room table. It was at first like any other morning. He was sitting in his regular chair at the head of the table, slouching forward, and hovering over the newspaper. He was turning the pages of the newspaper, and glancing over the articles describing the sinister occurrings of the last twenty-four hours—murder here, kidnapping there, riots, bomb-threats, burglary—enough shocking news to get any person depressed for the rest of the day. Next to the newspaper on the table lay his plate with the delicious breakfast that my mother served up fresh for us every morning. This morning it was "porota"—a type of thick, crusty, layered bread made from flour, a pinch of salt and lots of ghee. My father was ripping off the bread with his right hand and putting tiny pieces into his mouth, while he turned the newspaper with his left. After every couple of pieces he would take a sip from his steaming cup of milk tea. Every now and again, he would fumble with the copper-wired glasses neatly sitting at the arch of his nose, or rub the side of his moustache.

I put the finishing touches to my school attire and tied the shoe laces. I briskly ran a brush through my hair one more time before picking up my back-pack.

"Bye, Ammu!" I shouted towards my mother who was still in the kitchen preparing breakfast.

Walking past my father on the way out the door, I got a sudden urge to give him a hug. I don't remember ever hugging my dad, even when I was younger. He was really not the type to openly show affection. Hugs or kisses made him really uncomfortable. So it was just not the thing we did in our household—hug our parents when we felt like it, or god forbid, kiss them. My mum was a bit more affectionate and would not mind if we gave her a hug, but to my dad it was inconceivable.

Restraining myself from wanting to give him a hug, I instead sung out, "See you in a few days, Abbu. Enjoy your trip!"

As I looked at him one last time, I had this unknown feeling overcome me. It's something that I had never felt before, and hoped never to feel again. It's a thought that randomly occupied my mind; I don't know where it came from or the lead up to it. "This may be the last time that you ever glance at his face." *It scared me to think something so random but I decided to listen to it for a second. As I prepared to shut the door behind me, I made sure to hold my gaze for as long as I could and have the image of him engraved in my memory forever. There he was still looking at the newspaper with his head down when he mumbled, "See you soon."*

Later that day when I returned home from school my mother said that my father had called earlier from the office to say he had forgotten to take with him the pair of slippers he wore around the house. He was considering whether to drop by around five in the afternoon, before leaving with his colleagues for the trip, and pick those up. I was adamant that he should. I thought of every possible reason why that exact pair of slippers was going to be invaluable to him during this trip, why he must come home and pick those up. I asked my mother to call him back and tell him exactly what I had said to her, hoping to convince him that it was important for him to pick up the sandals. As ridiculous as it may have sounded, I just needed to make sure I could see him one more time before he set out on this journey. I had absolutely no idea why I was feeling this way but I knew it had to be done.

Much to my disappointment, around five in the afternoon, my father decided that he could do without the slippers and called to say that he was too caught up at work to be able to drop by before leaving. He would have to do without them. He said his goodbye to my mother and hung up.

As I now sat in this empty little room with just my aunt who had broken the horrible news of my father's death, it suddenly dawned on me. I don't know how I could have known that this was going to happen, but somehow I did. Call it intuition, call it sixth-sense or whatever the psychics were calling it these days, but I knew. I knew that my father was to go on a trip, which to everyone else at the time was for less than a week, but to me—it was for eternity.

Chapter 3

I left the study room in a daze and headed over to the master bedroom. As I walked with small footsteps, I was suddenly conscious of all the eyes around the house watching me, watching my reaction to the news that had just been broken to me. Some of the people I recognised as either my relatives or my father's colleagues, but some I had never seen before. Regardless of who they were, they looked at me with sympathy or even pity. I didn't have the strength or the desire to talk to them or be polite towards them; I just wanted to get to my mother. As I neared the door of the master bedroom, I picked up my pace, rushed through it and encased her with my arms. She wrapped her arms around me and we both started to sob in unison. I could hear words of comfort coming from those around us but I couldn't make out what they were saying. My mind was a thousand miles away.

What had happened? What did I ever do to deserve this? What did my mother ever do wrong to deserve to be widowed at an age when she barely had any visible wrinkles on her face? *What was I going to tell my younger sister, the apple of my father's eye, and only seven years of age, who was finally beginning to have more meaningful conversations with her father than "Hi daddy, what are you doing"? The one who used to hide his glasses every morning thinking it would stop him from going to work that day, not realising that all it did was only delay him a little?*

With that thought hanging over my head, suddenly I snapped out of it, and realised someone needed to tell my older sister who was still at school. She deserved to know right away and I wanted to share the pain with her, as we had often shared many experiences in the past—good or bad. I asked one of my uncles to drive me to the school so I could fetch her. I wanted to be the one to break the news to her gently, and to provide her the support she would need. When I got to the school I headed straight for the library knowing that's where she was hiding, trying to get some school work out of the way. As I peeked through the library door, I saw the librarian sitting perched up in her high chair.

"Can you please tell me where Sumara is?" I emphasized, "It is really urgent."

"The last time I saw her, she was at one of the tables in the back row, buried in her books," offered the librarian.

I moved swiftly through the lines of books stacked up against the walls and headed towards the back of the room. I soon noticed her with her head down; her eyes squinted, scribbling something on the open notebook in front of her.

"You have to come home, right now. It's urgent." I panted as I rushed to her.

She looked up at me with annoyance in her eyes. "I can't. I need to get this done now. Go home, I'll follow soon."

"No, no, really Sumara, it's urgent. You must come now." I pleaded.

"Go away. I'll be there when I'm done," she said forcefully.

I blurted unwillingly, "Sumara, dad is dead."

She looked up at me, not knowing what to make of the words that just rolled out of my tongue.

"Sumara, dad has passed away." I re-iterated, with tears streaming down my face as I slowly walked towards her.

She stared at me, numb. "Are you messing with me?" Her voice quivered, as it started to sink in by the look in my eyes that this was anything but a nasty joke played by a younger sibling on the older.

I bent down halfway until my shoulders came down to the same level as hers, as she leaned back in her chair, and held her for a moment. Slowly she composed herself, stood up and gathered her books from across the table in front of her. I helped her tuck in the loose pages of notes into the exercise book and drop it in her back pack. Walking towards the library exit was like a painful slow motion scene from the movies, as the questioning looks from the gazes of those pitiful eyes around us continued to burn holes through thin air.

We soon stepped outside into the hallway, ran down the stairs, cut through the soccer field and headed towards the shelter of the car that brought me to the school to pick up my sister. All the way home, neither of us said a word. We sat there silently, still not convinced that this was reality. My body felt numb, my heart heavy, and my throat choking back the tears that could fall like a monsoon pour if allowed to fall freely.

The rest of that day was a blur. It couldn't have been any less than a gigantic roller coaster ride that seemed to bring on an ocean of ups and downs. Sometimes I felt as though I was losing my mind. One minute I would think of my father and of something he would have said or done, and breakdown uncontrollably, the next someone would have said something remotely funny and I would have broken into a fit of laughter. The number of times I had some of the mourners look at me strangely due to my absurd behaviour of laughing out loud the day I got the news of my father passing away was more than I could count with both hands.

It was stranger trying to explain to my younger sister, Romana, what had happened. The fact that she was still a child, a child who didn't understand the concept of death, let alone realise all those around us would leave us someday, only made the task at hand that much harder. My mother, when she finally managed to get a grip and let out a few words, sat my little sister down next to her on the bed to try to explain to her calmly what had happened. That daddy had gone away yesterday to a work trip with his colleagues. He was on the stage making a speech to hundreds of employees at a site far, far away from home. The excitement of it all got too much to him and he felt sick, so he collapsed. She tried to describe the circumstances to help my sister understand the situation better.

She didn't say what was the ominous truth:

"Your daddy's poor heart just gave in. He fell to the floor while in front of an audience, clutched his chest, but they took too long to call an ambulance. By the time the ambulance had finally arrived and could take him to the hospital to revive his dying heart, he had already kicked the bucket. He went away with a duffle bag on his shoulder but will be returning in a body bag. Are you OK, sweetheart?"

No matter how cautiously or logically my mother phrased it, Romana just didn't understand. Every morning for months afterwards she would wake up and check the front door to see if her beloved father had returned, carrying with him presents for her, from wherever he had gone away to. May be it was because we never allowed her to see his corpse when it was finally brought home for the funeral, the realisation didn't hit that he would never return. It took a whole day for his body to be sent from where he had passed away, hundreds of miles away from home, to where he belonged. There was no air route, so he could not be flown back. The only way was to be driven back for hours in a van in the heat, made worse by terrible traffic conditions. By the time we finally got a chance to say goodbye, he was barely recognisable. I remembered his face being black like charcoal and swollen like a full-blown balloon. That day, as I looked at the face of this man who had been my idol in life, the person I always looked up to and never wanted to disappoint, I promised myself to fulfil his wishes and to look after those he loved the most.

I had also promised myself that I would never *ever* cry again as much as I did that day.

Chapter 4

The lights were turned off as I lay quietly on my bed. I dragged the pillow across my face, with my left arm over it to hold it in place, as I tried to concentrate and get to sleep. I had an early start tomorrow, with a long day ahead at work. Important meetings in the morning, and presentations in the afternoon. Plenty of preparation in between. I needed to be fresh and focussed. It was going to be a significant one in the early days of my career. I zoned in to the darkness and tried to clear my head of any thoughts which might keep me up for longer. At least half an hour would have passed when my eyelids finally started to feel heavy.

Ringgggg.

My mobile phone started to go off. The noise of the ring sounded more annoying than the tone of my alarm in early mornings. I slowly moved up my right arm across to the bed-side table and picked up the phone. It was my fiancé calling.

"Hi baby", I said groggily as I answered the phone. "Are you home from work yet?"

My fiancé lived in his own apartment just up the road, while I stayed with my family in a townhouse a few hundred meters away. We had been engaged for almost a year by then, but still had not moved in together. Not officially anyway, even though we spent quite a lot of time at his apartment. Not that we specially cared about what others in the Bangladeshi community might think, but we didn't want to embarrass our families. They still had reservations about a boy and a girl living together before getting married, so we didn't want to complicate matters by disrespecting their beliefs. Even though moving in at this point in time would have been the most logical choice. It would have definitely made more sense financially, given my fiancé was still completing his university education and often struggled to cope with all the household expenses on his own. I tried to chip in whenever I could—do the grocery shopping now and then, help out with the bills, and even sometimes cover part of the rent. It seemed logical to me given I spent a lot of my time at his apartment. However, it did mean that I was paying for those things twice—both at the house I was sharing with my family and at his. Twice the bills and twice the rent, but a small price to pay to keep everyone happy.

I was at my house tonight, coveting some uninterrupted sleep. My fiancé worked until late on Sunday nights which meant if I wanted to get some decent sleep, I was better off staying at my place. I chose to do so tonight given the big day ahead tomorrow. It wasn't anything unusual for us. We had learnt to work out what suited our circumstances best. And not always through discussion or forward planning.

"Why are you at yours tonight? Why aren't you here?" An angry spiteful voice on the other side of the line caught me by surprise. I was still too sleepy to fully comprehend the conversation that was about to unfold.

The roaring on the other end continued. "You useless bitch. What are you doing at your house? Come over here right now."

The voice sounded like a murmur to me a million miles away. It sounded very real and yet very distant at the same time. I don't know if it was the daze I was in or my desperate search for a peaceful night's sleep, I hung up the phone on him in my drowsy state.

Ringggggggggggggg.... The phone rang again, sounding much louder and meaner than before.

"Did you just hang up on me?" The words echoed in my ear, the voice even angrier than before. "Did you go shopping today? There is no toilet paper. I asked you to buy toilet paper, you worthless piece of shit."

I started to open my mouth to respond, but no words came out. Still in a state of sub-consciousness, somewhere between the land of the awake and the land of the asleep, I found myself asking why I would even consider responding to such atrocity. I hung up, put my phone to mute and dropped my head back in the previous position. Thirty seconds later I could feel the phone vibrating. I couldn't switch it off because I had set the alarm on my phone to wake me up the next morning. I let it vibrate. Once, twice, three times. He was trying to call me.

Finally he gave up. Another vibration—a shorter one this time. A text message came through.

"Pick up the phone! Call me back right now!!" it read.

Even as a text message the words seemed mean. They echoed his anger. I could visualise his fair cheeks turning red, flustered; the veins on his forehead throbbing so hard they looked green and protruded.

A few minutes passed. Another vibration. *"If you don't get your ass over here right now, we are over!"*

This was nothing new to me. I had often heard him utter those words before. Not all those exact words but the last three, quite often, in different situations. Most things with him ended with an ultimatum—if things didn't go his way or he didn't get what he wanted. At the start of our relationship, when I was much younger, more naïve and more afraid to lose, those words always caught me out. They made me sad, subdued and often obey his wishes—depending on if I was feeling vulnerable or rebellious. Over time my reaction to those words was less and less drastic. They became less effective, causing distance between us rather than serve its intended purpose.

Today, five strong-willed words floated around in my head as I read the last message and put the phone back down on the bed-side table.

"That suits me just fine".

And just like that I made the decision to call off my engagement and break free from the five-year-long relationship that caused me to shed more tears than I had ever thought possible. Enough was enough, and it was time for me to cut my losses. It took me all these years to finally conjure up the courage to take a stand that I should have taken possibly at least three years ago. But as they say, "better late than never".

Waking up the next morning, the strangest feeling engulfed me. A wave of grief, followed by that of relief, followed by anger, despair and more grief. I didn't know how to feel, all I knew was that for now I needed to keep going. If it meant pretending to not have just gone through one of the biggest changes in my life, then that's what it had to be. In order to gather the energy to keep going and not to have the world collapse around me, I needed to forget for the moment what had happened while at the same time stand my ground.

For almost a year I had been standing at these cross-roads. Whilst all the plans were being put in place for me to go right, last night I took the turn to the left, and at a point of no return. As the events unfolded to the lead up to our engagement almost a year ago, I contemplated whether or not this was the right choice for either of us. Whether or not we were really meant for each other as we had led ourselves to believe and if we could stay together forever. Did we feel the way we felt about each other when we first started dating four years before that? Or were we kidding ourselves thinking this was the right course of action simply because society had taught us so? The urge that you feel inside of you, something churning within when you look at someone, when you want them to touch you and caress you—was that meant to last forever or did that wither with time?

I knew I loved him, but so much had changed. There was something missing. What was amiss was lost over time as my heart or my head couldn't bare it anymore. The pain, the suffering, the consistent inconsistency, and worst of all, the doubt. Not doubt over whether I loved him, but more over whether he truly loved me. If I was only to believe his words when he was angry, it was guaranteed that he didn't love me at all. If I was to only believe those when he was happy, it meant nothing in the world could ever tear us apart. He said he loved me, he said he wanted to spend the rest of his life by my side, that he would die without me . . . so he proposed. But if I just put my hands over my ears and used only my eyes to see his actions, then his actions too sent me contradicting messages. If actions spoke louder than words, then I would not have a clue in the world on where he stood. On a good day he would shower me with kisses, hug me, cuddle me and even buy me something nice out of the blue. Yet sometimes, on a terribly bad day, when his bare hand would cut through the air and land on my barren cheek—the action spoke otherwise. It hurt like hell, and not just physically.

It wasn't always like this, and I don't even know when it got this way. There was a time when it was all about being in the moment and being only with each other. There was an attraction that would drive anyone mad. May be that was the problem, it was too passionate and that drove us mad. Or maybe I was too blind to see what was right in front of me the whole time. Only if you could get inside someone's head and know for sure the truth about how they really felt. Life would be a lot less complex. Yes, may be a lot less interesting too but at least you would be in the know. There was nothing worse than not knowing. Well . . . not at least to me, anyway.

Chapter 5

"*H*ello, is that you?" I asked excitedly at the speaker of the telephone I held with my right hand. With my left I clutched onto my handbag. My luggage rested next to me on the ground. I was standing at the phone booth outside the "Arrivals" lounge at the Melbourne International Airport.

"Where the heck have you been? I have been trying to get in touch with you for over two days. I was worried sick. Where are you and what the heck is going on?" My boyfriend almost screamed into the phone from the other end of the line, his voice full of anxiety.

"Guess where I am?" I teased him a little longer.

"Where?" He probed, sounding a little confused.

"I am at the Melbourne Airport. I am here!" I exclaimed.

"No way! What? You are here? Really? When did you get in? Why didn't you tell me? Don't go anywhere. Stay right there. I am coming to pick you up. I am getting out of bed right now; I will leave the house right away. Stay there!" The words gushed from his mouth.

He sounded like an overly-excited schoolboy who had just been handed his new toy at Christmas. This was exactly the reaction I was hoping for. We hadn't seen each other in four months and I was supposed to be away for another four. I was travelling around the world. This trip was a dream of mine, and I had my itinerary planned out months in advance, even before we had met each other. All the hotels were booked, every leg of the journey paid for. I was to spend a few months in the USA visiting my friends, and relatives who had migrated there a few years earlier. Then a tour through Europe, followed by one in Asia, before I eventually returned home. I had even taken a semester off university to be able to accommodate this trip. Then I met him.

I didn't know how we were going to feel about each other or where the relationship would head. It was only supposed to be a few dates at first. I only dated him for just two months before heading overseas. We tried to break it off before I was to leave, but it ended up being a night full of dramas, with the decision made that we would continue whatever this was, to see where it led us. There was just something there. Soon enough though all the conversations over the phone got tedious and I could hear it in his voice that he was hurting. So one night, while lying in my bed somewhere in a small Swedish town, I just decided to catch the next flight back home. It would only be a small sacrifice to make. I could always live that dream of travelling to the countries I hadn't been to yet in the future, and possibly with him. For now, I needed to give this a chance with the guy who made me feel things I had not experienced before. I thought it was still too pre-mature to call it love, but it felt special.

I hung up the phone and picked up the handle to my suitcase with my right hand. I had an hour to kill before he would arrive. He lived quite far away from the airport and I lived about twenty minutes away. I was better off taking a taxi, but I knew it would mean a lot to him if I just stayed put so that he was able to pick me up. I headed to the washroom. I looked into the mirror as I walked in. I was wearing a pair of light blue jeans and a white T-shirt I had picked up in Stockholm. The T-shirt read "Dallas". I had been to Dallas just a few weeks earlier, so when I saw this T-shirt at a small boutique store in Stockholm I thought it was quite fitting that I buy it. It stood out against the contrast of my darker skin tone. My hair had grown a fair bit over the last four months, and reached past my shoulders. I pulled it up into a ponytail. After a seventeen-hour journey on the plane I looked as tired as I felt. I pulled out my eye shadow from the handbag and applied some to lighten up my eyes. I applied some mascara and a bit of lip gloss. I was ready to meet the boy I had dated longer over the phone then in person, but it felt like we had known each other for eternity.

I walked out of the washroom and found a chair in the corner in the lounge area, as I anxiously waited. My nerves were all over the place. I was excited to be seeing him soon but didn't know what to expect. I wondered if he would be able to spot me straight away as he walked into the airport hall. I wondered if he had changed much from how I remembered him to be four months ago. By now back in the lounge, all the passengers who arrived with me had found their loved ones and left. The arrival hall was nearly empty, only a few people hung about in the distance. Some gave me inquisitive looks, wondering why I was still there, sitting in the corner with my luggage, all by myself. I tried to shrug off their glances.

I grabbed my diary from the hand-luggage and shuffled through its pages. It had scribbles on each page of the city I had been to or small notes of my adventure of the day. One such note read: *"Hired a car with my cousins to drive from Los Angeles to San Francisco. Made a stop-over at Lake Tahoe—amazing view! Lucky that I convinced my cuz to get insurance, he drove the car into the pole while reversing to park in the drive-away—when we had already reached our destination nonetheless . . . LOL! San Fran was so picturesque!"*

I smiled at myself and leafed through to another page: *"I would have loved to stay a little longer and take that boat cruise from Sweden to Finland but this is the only flight available to Melbourne in two months! I am sure I made the right choice."* I flipped through to the last note in the diary written less than twenty-four hours ago: *"Long transit at Heathrow on the way back home but I love this airport. Keeping myself occupied checking out the shops. Bought some Quality Street chocolates for mum, her favourite!"*

"I can't believe what I have done!" I exclaimed to myself at the realisation that I had cut my 'around the world' trip short for a guy. I was supposed to still be in Europe, making my way through several destinations before finally heading to Paris for New Year's celebrations. This was the same guy who pursued me for months before I finally gave in; the same guy who tried to break up with me twice before I left but couldn't do it. He didn't want me to feel like I was tied down to something while I should be roaming the earth free. He contradicted himself in a lot of ways. First he wouldn't take 'no' for an answer when I said it wasn't good timing to date him. Then he wouldn't take 'yes' for an answer when I tried to reassure him that I could handle being in a relationship during our time apart, *if he could.* Two days before my departure was the last attempt he made at trying to let me go.

It had been a gloomy day in Melbourne, with an overshadowed sky and round-the-clock pouring rain. We barely caught a glimpse of the sun all day. So when it finally set, it felt as though it was still hiding behind the clouds as it had all day. I couldn't tell night apart from day. I had just finished my dinner with the family when my boyfriend called to say he was in his car, parked just outside my home. He hadn't called, sent a sms, or left a voicemail to let me know that he might be dropping by. I was shocked but excited. I wanted to see him as many times as I could before I left. It was impossible to believe how we felt about each other in such a short period of time. All the both of us knew was that when we were together it felt as though we had known each other forever. It felt right. We enjoyed each other's company. We shared our deepest darkest secrets. We talked non-sense. We talked about the future. We laughed, cried, kissed, and cuddled. We were just comfortable being with one another.

I tried to find an umbrella before I stepped out, but I was feeling very impatient. My heart suddenly started to race at a hundred kilometres per hour. I didn't want to keep him waiting. I looked for a minute in the closet next to the door, but not being able to find one instantly, just ran outside in the rain. I saw his car parked a couple of doors down, with the headlights turned on and the engine still running. I sprinted towards it—his 1987 Toyota Camry dark blue sedan. The car was old and had hundreds of kilometres on it but this was all he could afford to drive for now. Since our first date he had been talking about his dream car—still manual transmission but something with a bit more muscle, a bit more rev. May be a V8 Holden Commodore. "I would change the 19 inch alloy wheels to chrome wheels and add body kit", *he would say as the Commodore advertisements would come on the television or as he watched his favourite programme Top Gear. As soon as he noticed me hustling towards the car in the pouring rain, he held the passenger's side door wide open. I jumped inside soaking wet, water dripping from me, head to toe. He first gave me a long passionate kiss, then pulled away. He turned off the headlights and the car engine. It was deadly silent inside the car for at least a whole minute. His face was solemn.*

"Baby, what's wrong?" I probed.

"You need to go into this adventure as you had planned. You need to do this single," he replied with a cracked voice.

"Huh? Why do you say that?" I was genuinely confused.

"You will meet a lot of interesting characters. Lots of interesting guys. You can't have fun if you are with me."

I stared at him in astonishment for a split second, then burst out laughing.

"Do you seriously think that this is what the trip is about?" I paused. "I planned this trip because I wanted to see the world. I wanted to see the places that I had read about in my Geography class in school. I wanted to get a taste of the cultures I had read about in history books. It was about experiencing what fascinated me during my childhood. It was about being able to live it. It wasn't about guys. If I just wanted to have fun with guys, I might as well stay here!"

"You are just saying that," he mumbled with his head down, not sounding very confident.

"Baby, it might have been a different scenario if I wasn't with you right now, but I can't do this to you. I wouldn't." I emphasized. "It's my weakness. I am too loyal. Got it from my dad. I couldn't even think about someone else while I am with you."

I meant what I said with all my heart.

Seeing he didn't flinch a bit at my comment, I continued, "Let me tell you a story. I would have been just about ten years old. I was in primary school at the time. One day during lunch break, a fight broke out between my best friend and another classmate. Can't even remember what it was about. Might have been just a small misunderstanding between kids. Anyway, my best friend was really upset. There was a bit of pushing and shoving. She got hurt. Very mildly. You know what I did?"

"What?"

"I didn't care what it was about or about the fact that it had nothing to do with me. All I knew was that my friend was hurting. So I stood up for her. I told off the other girl. I just scared her out of her wits, intimidated her with my height and a stern voice. I said if she ever messed with my friend again, she would also be messing with me. I threatened her that she will have no friends left if she didn't get her act together. I think my height would have done the trick. I was always taller than average amongst the girls in my class growing up." I giggled.

He seemed to consider his thoughts for a moment, trying to articulate it.

"Out of sight, out of mind." He finally said.

"For you or for me? I am more of a 'Absence makes the heart grow fonder' kinda gal." I confessed.

We sat there silently for a while. He stared into the distance through the car windshield. I watched him, placing a gentle kiss on his left cheek now and then.

An hour and a quarter had passed by. I put my diary away from where I had pulled it out. Suddenly as I looked up, I saw this six-foot tall figure approaching through the doors at the far end of the hall. He was wearing a pair of dark blue jeans and a black jacket. He looked much thinner than the boy I was expecting. My stomach started to flutter. My hands clenched. I couldn't see the face clearly given the distance but I knew who it was. Our eyes met as he came a little closer and I saw his brighten up like the hot summer's day that it was. It felt like one of those scenes out of a romance novel when the boy and the girl met for the first time, or when long lost loves finally found each other. I could feel my heart pounding in my chest at a hundred miles an hour as I saw him break into a run to be able to get to me quicker.

A few moments later he was coming to a halt and picking me up off the ground. He squeezed me so tight I could barely breathe. I was showered with kisses on my cheek and my forehead. I held his unshaven face in my hands and lay a big one on him. We didn't want to let each other go. It was only the dawning eyes of strangers around us that eventually brought us back to reality. As we walked side by side clinging to each other with our arms around the other's waist and headed towards the airport car park, it felt like the start of something great. He looked into my eyes with a sense of longing as though all he wanted was to seclude me from the rest of the world so I was only his to keep. My pounding chest had calmed a little, replaced by a smile on my face from ear to ear. I was glad to have made the hasty decision of returning home early and being rewarded with the excitement on the face of someone I was starting to care a lot about. We were on the top of the world and nothing could tear us apart!

Chapter 6

*M*y boyfriend was ecstatic about being able to celebrate my birthday with me, as was I. This would be the first birthday we celebrated together with hopes of plenty more to come. I didn't want to come across as a demanding little princess, a high-maintenance girlfriend, so I didn't ask if he had made any plans. Some of my friends, who were quite delighted to have me back early for my birthday as well, had pulled together a small gathering at the last minute. Since my boy had to work on the afternoon of my birthday, I decided to hang out with them while he was working but invited him to join us when he had finished. It was just a simple barbeque in the park close to where he was working, so I was looking forward to having him there as soon as he could be.

My friends were taking turns at the barbeque, cooking up a storm—lamb chops, marinated chicken breasts, steaks, vegetarian patties, grilled vegetables . . . plenty to go around. I wasn't allowed to lift a finger. I was happy to take it all in and appreciate all the familiar faces that surrounded me, telling them stories of my adventure abroad. Even so, now and then, my heart would pull a string and I would look at my watch, wondering how much longer it would be till I saw him. By then, it had already been a couple of hours since we first fired up the barbeque grill.

He should be here any minute now, I thought.

He was about to finish work in a few minutes, and it wouldn't take him more than five minutes to drive down to the park. Any minute now. I was counting down the seconds. Five minutes passed, then ten, then twenty. I pulled my mobile out of my handbag and dialled his number.

"Hey baby, where are you?"

"I am at home. Where are you?" he replied with some distress in his voice.

"I am here in the park with my friends. We are waiting for you before we get started. Will you be long?" I enquired.

"I don't know. I will come if I can. You get started without me," was his brief response and then he hung up.

I started to worry. Is he ok? Did something happen at work? Is he upset? If so, why?

I dialled his number. No answer. It went straight to voicemail. I left a brief message voicing my concerns and asked him to give me a call back. One of my friends asked if my boyfriend would be long given they were about to finish up with the barbecue.

"The meat will be getting cold," informed the one to have taken charge at the grill.

"He is held up, and asked us to get started without him. You guys go ahead." I sheepishly responded, unsure of what else to tell them.

The meat, the salad and the bread were laid out on the bench underneath a tree in the park. It took us only about half an hour to finish gobbling down all the grilled delights. We wiped our mouths and patted our tummies like satisfied ogres. There was still no response on my mobile—no reply message, no voicemail, no call.

I tried his number again. No response.

The sun had already set and the air was starting to get chilly even though it was the middle of summer. We needed to gather our things and head indoors. I didn't have an explanation for my friends regarding the whereabouts of my mystery man. So I decided to head over with them to one of their houses and send him a text to let him know where we were. Hopefully he would receive it and turn up there.

As nice as it was to be with my friends, my heart was breaking. It wasn't so much just the fact that I was missing his presence—even though I was—it was more the uncertainty and awkwardness with which our conversation had ended. Just a few days ago he was telling me how glad he was to have me back early; to be able to celebrate my birthday with me, but how sorry he was that he couldn't take time off work. So I was going to hang out with my friends until he finished work and we could do something together afterwards. Something special. It was going to be perfect.

After an hour of hanging around at my friend's I decided it was time I headed home. I was feeling a little sad and confused, unable to get in touch with my boyfriend. One of my friends decided to give me a lift home. I was about an hour and a quarter away from where I lived. After what felt like the longest drive of my life, still jet-lagged from the trip abroad, and a somewhat eventful day, I finally arrived home a little after midnight.

As I turned the key into the lock of the front door, I heard footsteps approaching the door. My heart thudded against my chest. I could not help but silently hope that it was him. I opened the door. My face dropped.

It was Sumara standing near the doorway.

"He was here. You just missed him," my sister said. "He left a cake for you and some gifts. I put the gifts on your bed."

I didn't know how to feel. Happy? Sad? Confused? Ecstatic?

I marched across the hallway, into the kitchen on my right, and opened the refrigerator door. Taking out the cake from the second shelf from the top, I put it gently on the kitchen bench top. I opened the lid.

There it was the prettiest cake I had ever seen. It was a heart-shaped cake, covered with red-icing and the words "Happy 19th Birthday My Love" scribbled in white on top. I was perplexed. It was the nicest thing anyone had ever done for me. I thought to myself, *"May be that's exactly why he was acting all strange. He just wanted to leave me a surprise."*

I gently put the lid back on and put the cake back in the fridge.

I skipped to my bedroom, in anticipation of what lay on my bed. I found myself stunned when I saw what it was.

Over a dozen of the most exquisite yellow roses, tied neatly in a bunch with a matching ribbon.

I leaped towards my bed and picked up the card that lay next to the roses.

"To the most special person in my life. Happy birthday! Yours truly." It read.

I was as impressed as I was ecstatic. I felt spoilt but loved. I couldn't wait to call him and tell him how much I appreciated the gesture.

I reached into my handbag and grabbed my mobile. I dialled his number. It rang four times, then nothing. It didn't even go to his voicemail. I tried one last time. Someone was definitely hanging up on me at the other end. Out of courtesy, if not anything else, I thought I should send him a 'thank you' note. I typed the following into my phone and sent him a text message.

"Hey, tried to call u several times but can't get through. Just got the gifts u left me. Thank u sooooo much. The roses are beautiful & love the cake. Wish u had stayed a lil longer. Sorry I missed u. Can't wait 2 see u. Call me back."

After sending the message, I put the mobile on top of my bedside table and picked up the roses. I walked over to the kitchen and opened the door of the cupboard under the sink. Taking out a medium-sized white vase, I half-filled it with water. I put down the vase on the kitchen bench-top and took off the ribbon from around the bunch of roses. Leaving the ribbon on the bench-top, I dipped the stems into the water in the vase and let the flowers hang on the side from the mouth of the vase. I took the vase of roses back into my room and laid it down on the bedside table. Then changing into my night-gown, I ducked under the covers on my bed.

I fell asleep thinking of how the day had turned out. It was supposed to be the perfect day, spent with all my favourite people—those who cared about me and those who I cared about. Instead it was one filled with anticipation and uncertainty. The gifts were a nice gesture, but being hung up on, or not being contacted, definitely was not. I just couldn't shake the thought that I had cut my holiday short because he missed me, because he had sounded more and more depressed on the phone every day, but now on my birthday, there was no sight of him. No spending time together, no being in each others' arms. I was alone, and confused.

I woke up early the next morning still wondering why there was no response from my so-called boyfriend. I knew he would still be asleep. His daily routine was to go to bed in the middle of the night and wake up just after mid-day. If he had an early class at the university, he would make an effort to get up five minutes before the class and drive like a maniac to get there. Some days he won't even bother trying.

The morning passed quickly as I kept myself busy with little chores around the house. As soon as it hit mid-day I dialled the number that now seemed to roll off the tip of my fingers.

"Hello?" said a voice groggily at the other end.

"Hi, it's me. I had been trying to reach you all day yesterday. Thank you for the gifts. Why didn't you pick up the phone?"

"Why should I? You were too busy with your friends," he replied in a dissatisfied tone of voice.

"What do you mean?" I asked stunned. "I thought we agreed I was going to hang out with my friends until you finished work and then you will join us. I had no idea you had other plans."

"You seem to care more about what your friends want. I came over last night and you were still out with your friends. I wanted to wish you happy birthday and bring you the gifts in person at midnight. I never wanted to join them. I wanted time with just you, alone." There was still some aggression in his voice.

"I had no idea! Why didn't you tell me? I can't know what you are thinking. It's just a small misunderstanding." After a small pause, I continued, "What are you doing today? Come over to my house. We will cut the cake together."

"I don't know," he said firmly.

"Don't be mad. Come on! Come over." I responded in a pleading voice.

"I'll be there around three," he replied in a much softer tone and then hung up.

The door-bell rang promptly at three in the afternoon. His face was freshly shaven and he had on a crisply ironed white-and-blue checked shirt. As I opened the door, he leaned forward and gave me a small peck on the cheek. It was a gesture to suggest that he had started to calm down, but was still a little upset at how the events unfolded the day before. Therefore, no kiss.

I led him through the hallway into the living room. He dropped himself onto a sofa and spread his long legs in front of him onto the carpet. I asked if he wanted anything to drink, and bringing him the glass of water he requested, I sat down next to him.

"So, how are you doing?" I probed.

"Yeah, OK." He replied, hesitant to offer much more than that.

"Babe, I had no idea you had all these planned. Thank you so much. The flowers are beautiful. And the cake! Where did you order it from?"

"I requested the chef at my work to bake one for me and told him how I wanted it to be."

"Well, it's amazing. So thank you." I said as I planted a kiss on his cheek. "Let's go and get ourselves a few slices."

I got up from the sofa and he followed. We walked into the kitchen to get a taste of what he had brought in the night before. As I cut a couple of small slices of the cake onto two plates, I intended to find out more about the occurring of the night before. I was just thinking of how to politely bring up the topic again when finally, as we sat down with the plates onto the dining table, he burst out.

"I was really mad at you last night. I thought you came back early to spend more time with me. We were going to spend your birthday together. Was it too much to ask that you stay at home until I finish work and then we could have had the rest of the day together? Oh, no! You had to go off with your friends."

"But . . . I don't understand." I replied, caught off-guard. "We discussed it. We decided on it. What is the point of me hanging around here on my birthday if my friends had something planned and you were working? You should have said something before if you took an issue with this. You shouldn't have just hung up on me."

"I don't need to spell everything out for you," was his brief response.

"Well, let's face it. We are still trying to get to know and understand each other. For future reference, would you please just communicate a little better so I know what really is going on in your head?" I requested in an almost pleading voice.

He didn't respond, but just sat there quietly with his head down and a grim look on his face. I knew he was still upset about something more but this was all I was going to get out of him that day. We finished our slices of cake and dropped the plates into the kitchen sink. It was a beautiful day outside, so we decided to go for a walk in the park in close vicinity to my house.

As we stepped out onto the street, he put his arm around my waist. The day was warm. There were not many people around on the streets. It was quite a suburban neighbourhood. As we approached the park, there were a couple of children around ten years of age swinging on the swings. We walked in a circle around the park on the footpath. There was some small chit chat, but no further discussion of the night before.

After about an hour of spending time in the sun, we headed back to my house. He soon said goodbye and drove off, as he was working at the restaurant later that evening.

I was still in vacation and didn't have any classes. I had taken time off my part-time work before I went overseas. They were not expecting me back for another four months. However, it was too long a time to not be working. I would not have much to do around the house or otherwise, and it was better to have the income coming in as well. I called my manager at work and arranged to meet with him the following day.

Everyone at work was surprised by my return. I didn't want to explain the exact reasons for my early return, and left out the specifics. It was suffice to say those who knew of my boyfriend had figured out what the real reason might have been. Others just bought into my explanation that it had something to do with the family. I decided to work fewer hours to start off with as I settled back completely into the 'normal' lifestyle. I would work more hours than usual in a month's time, until my classes at the university resumed.

Working less hours initially also meant more time with my boyfriend. Given the distance we each had to travel to see each other, having more time at hand to do so was never a bad idea. He lived with a housemate who was almost never around, so if he was at home for too long by himself, he started to feel very lonely. I liked keeping him company. I enjoyed driving down to his house and spending time with him when neither of us was working. It also gave us more privacy than at my house. We shopped together, cooked together, ate together, watched TV together and even did some of the household chores whenever I spent a day at his house. Other times he would come and pick me up, and we would go to the movies, or out to dinner. We often went for long drives if it was a beautiful day. He loved driving and I loved the tranquillity.

We didn't spend a whole lot of time with large groups of friends often. Either our random schedules and theirs would not match up or he wasn't too keen on the idea. It wasn't to say that we never did it, but it was not as much as I would have liked. He always preferred time alone with me—we talked and laughed and shared stories of our lives before we met. We shared our dreams and ambitions. So for the moment, I was delighted to have him by my side and appreciated all our time together, as did he. The relationship was starting to get too serious too quickly, without either of us truly realising it.

Chapter 7

A stormy Saturday afternoon forced me to stay indoors. The air smelled of rain and dust. I was cuddled up in front of the television on one of the couches. My older sister was lying down on the other, with her body turned half-way towards the television, a book in her hand. My younger sister was on the floor on the carpet, sitting across from the unused fireplace with her paint-brush and a canvas. She was working on a painting she had started a year ago but never got around to finishing. The vicious storm compelled us to be indoors so she decided it was as good a day as any to try to complete her unfinished work. My mother was in the kitchen, as she usually would be when she was home after work on weekdays and during the weekends. She loved cooking for her family. There were special dishes for every occasion, and today she was cooking her storm specials. It normally consisted of *Khichuri*, a traditional Bangladeshi meal cooked with rice and lentils eaten while steaming hot, which she normally served up with egg omelettes or curries. Tonight it was chicken curry cooked with a lot of spices and potatoes.

I looked outside through the window. It was dark, hazy, and very windy. The window seal was making loud creepy noises as branches of trees struck against it. Loose leaves were floating about like rustling feathers. *"This is just the perfect day to be staying home"*, I thought to myself. During an advertisement break, I got out of the couch and walked over to the kitchen. I looked over my mum's shoulder to see what she was stirring on the stove. Just as I was about to leave, her mobile rang. She asked me to take the ladle from her hand, and ran to pick up her phone from the dining table. "Keep stirring!" she shouted as she left. I continued the motion as she showed me, to make sure the ingredients didn't get stuck to the bottom of the pot. Ten minutes later, she returned with a solemn face.

"Ammu, who was it?" I enquired.

"That was your uncle from Dhaka," she said in a very low voice.

"What's wrong?" I asked again.

"Your grand-father has just passed away," she replied.

"What? No way. When? How?" I asked without taking a breath.

"An hour ago."

I quickly dropped the ladle, switched off the stove, and hugged my mother. The both of us walked back to the living room where my sisters were watching the television. She sat down on the empty couch. I took my place next to her.

"Ammu, what is it?" Sumara asked.

"Grandpa has just passed away." I responded and then asked my mother, "How did it happen?"

"He had a stroke. It was very sudden. My father was already so old. I am glad he didn't suffer," my mother consoled herself.

"Are you okay, mummy?" Romana asked.

"Yes, I am fine," she responded as a single tear drop escaped her left eye.

Each of us took turns giving her a hug. We requested her not to worry about the cooking. I asked her to sit with us in the lounge room but she insisted she wanted to head back to the kitchen. Thinking she might want some time on her own, we let her leave. The three of us sat there solemnly for a few minutes. The news had come as a shock. Our grand-father was in his eighties. So it wasn't a shock as it would be if a young man had passed away, but it was still very sudden. He was old but remarkably healthy. We hadn't heard any news of him being sick. There were lots of incredible memories with him from our last visit to Bangladesh. He was a very wise man who taught us a lot about politics, culture, religion and history while we were living in Dhaka. Every summer we would stay at our grand-parents' house for a few weeks during the school holidays. Those weeks would always be some of the most incredible weeks of the year for me. It was fun and exciting. There were a few cousins living with my grand-parents. We would always hang out together and do crazy things that you do as teenagers, like sneak out in the middle of the night or prank call strangers at three in the morning. Our grand-mother would always scold us or punish us for being naughty but grand-father, never. He always spoilt us. He loved buying us matching dresses and giving us money to buy lollies. We adored him.

While my sisters and I reminisced our time with him, my mother stayed in the kitchen slaving away. I decided to go and have a look to see how she was coping. As I walked through the kitchen, I caught her wiping away her tears. She sniffed, and smiled like everything was normal.

"Mum, you are allowed to be upset. You can cry. You don't have to hide away all the time. It's okay you know." I said as I hugged her tight.

She burst out crying as she heard me utter those words. "I never got a chance to say goodbye!" she said as she wailed. "I always thought there was time. I have been putting off my Dhaka visit and now I'll never get to see him again!"

"I am so sorry, mummy." I responded clutching her tighter. "Let's go and sit down. Come on, please! We can finish this off for you later."

Seeing her cry gave me tears in my eyes. I pulled her away from the kitchen and walked her back to the living room. Romana ushered her to sit down and handed her a tissue. We surrounded her as she talked about the last encounter with her father. When she felt calmer, she asked Romana to bring the telephone. As Romana handed the phone to her, she dialled the number for her mother in Dhaka. While my sisters kept her company, I snuck away to my bedroom and sent a text message to my boyfriend to let him know the bad news. Two seconds later, he called.

"Baby, are you okay?" said the voice on the other end.

"A little sad, but okay. It hurts to see mum so upset. She is always so good at hiding her emotions. I am glad though that she let go today."

"Is it okay for me to come over?"

"Of course, if you wanted to. It's still so gloomy outside." The storm had somewhat subsided but the dark clouds indicated another possible round.

"It's fine. I will be over in an hour."

"Drive carefully!" I urged before hanging up.

I returned to the living room to ask my mother what needed to be done to finish cooking. After she relayed the instructions, I wandered over to the kitchen and continued as she suggested. Sumara joined me a minute later and asked if I needed any help. When

I responded it was all under control, she decided to make some salad. Romana stayed with mum and they talked more about our grand-father. She was so young when she last saw him; there wasn't much she remembered of him. She didn't have the good fortune of getting to know him as well as I or Sumara did. All she could remember was his face and the stories we had told her over the years.

An hour later, the door bell rang. By then, the food was prepared and served on the table. My mother didn't know an extra person would be joining us for dinner. I was a bit nervous about introducing the guest to her. It had come up during an earlier conversation with her that I had met someone, but I didn't have the pleasure of introducing him to my mother yet. I didn't know if this was the most appropriate day for their first introduction. I supposed it was as good a day as any. He wanted to be supportive and be there for us. I couldn't refuse. In my nervous state, I opened the front door. He was standing there with a bouquet of flowers. I asked him to come in.

"Hi." He said as he entered, then added nodding towards the flowers, "These are for your mum."

"That is *so* thoughtful of you!" I exclaimed.

I was touched at the gesture. I wanted to kiss him, but didn't, in case my mother saw us. It would be disrespectful. I led him to the living room and asked him to wait while I called my mother. My mum was praying in her bedroom. I knocked on the door.

"Come in!" she said.

"Ammu, there is someone here that I want you to meet."

"Who is it?" she asked curiously.

"He is waiting in the living room. Just come over when you are ready."

I left her to get changed into something proper to welcome guests in. Five minutes later she joined us. As soon as my boyfriend saw her enter the room, he stood up.

"Ammu, this is . . . you know . . ."

My boyfriend decided to take the range. "It is so lovely to finally meet you. I am so sorry for your loss," he said sympathetically, handing my mother the bouquet.

"I am delighted to meet you too. Thank you for the flowers. They are beautiful!" she responded taking the bouquet from his hand.

"Here Ammu, give me the flowers. I will put these in a vase. Have a sit."

I left them to chat while I put the flowers in a vase. It was an odd mix of flowers, yet quite a beautiful bouquet. Still feeling a little nervous, but calmer than before, I walked back into the living room with the vase. I placed the vase in the centre of the coffee table. It looked like my mother and my boyfriend were getting along just fine. I quietly breathed a sigh of relief.

"May be we should start dinner?" I suggested.

"Yes, let's head to the dining table." My mother agreed.

We accompanied her as she stood up and walked towards the dining room. I called out for Sumara and Romana to join us. I had introduced Sumara to my boyfriend just a few weeks after we had started dating. I couldn't keep it a secret from her. It was almost as if I needed her approval even though I wasn't directly asking for it. Romana, on the other hand, didn't know he existed. I introduced her as she entered the room.

"This is Romana, my younger sister."

"I have heard so much about you." He said to Romana, then seeing Sumara enter the room added, "How are you, Sumara apu?"

"Very well, thanks. So good to see you again."

"You too." He said pulling out a chair to take a seat.

The rest of us grabbed a chair each and followed suit. As everyone chit-chatted away, I looked around the dining table. Finally, it felt complete. It was the beginning of an era. Our family had lost someone important that day but gained someone new. I smiled at my mother in contentment as she started to serve us the *Khichuri*. As if almost in sync, she smiled back.

Chapter 8

New Year's Eve soon approached bringing with it the usual hype and anticipation of how to farewell one year and welcome another. This was going to be our first New Year's Eve celebration together as a couple, much like how many other things were our first together that year. The plan was to start off with dinner, then meet up with my family and head towards the city centre to watch the fireworks display at midnight. Until that year, I had been celebrating New Year's Eve either with my family or my friends or both. This was the first time I was bringing a boy along. I did not want my family, especially my mum, to think I was a different person altogether now that I was seriously dating someone. If I was to go off on my own and celebrate just with him, I knew how my family would take it. Not so much my sisters, but more my mum being left alone to celebrate on her own. I often felt more obliged than usual to keep her company during festive times. May be I was trying to over-compensate for my father's absence in her life. My boyfriend's parents, on the other hand, still lived in Bangladesh. Otherwise I was sure it would have ended up being a huge family affair.

The dinner was exquisite. It was at an Italian restaurant on the way to the city centre. Another thing we had in common—our love of food, especially Italian. The neighbourhood where we had our dinner reservation was well-known for its Italian influences. The street packed with restaurants, cafes, ice cream parlours and boutique stores, famously known as Lygon Street, was a favourite amongst the locals. A hearty serving of a bowl of risotto for him and a plate full of delicious spaghetti marinara for me was enough to make us content on how the night had started out.

After our coveted meal, we decided to walk to the street corner where my mum and my sisters were to join us for the rest of the evening, leaving our car parked near Lygon Street. Finding parking in the city was going to be a nightmare. Nor would we want to risk some drunken party-goer scratching our car or smashing a window due to expected senselessness on the night. Not that such behaviour was common in Melbourne; we just didn't want to take any chances. It was about ten in the evening when we finally left the restaurant. The streets were starting to fill up with all those who intended to watch the fireworks from a location near the main train station of the city, Flinders Street Station, with a good view of the display, or from the bank of the Yarra River.

At about quarter past, I received a text message from my mother saying they were going to be running a little late. There were still many people trying to catch the trams to get into the city for the midnight celebrations. It was harder to get onto the trams than on a normal weekend evening, and it was not unusual that the journey would take longer than anticipated. However, by ten thirty they still had not arrived. I decided to tell my mother that we would walk down to the riverbank and try to find us a nice spot to sit down at. They should give me a call when they arrived at a specified location. I would go and meet them to bring them to the reserved spot.

By the time my boyfriend and I finally headed to the riverbank, it was about an hour till midnight. Most of the ground was already covered with mats and picnic baskets. We still managed to push ourselves through the crowd and sit by the river. We had a perfect view ahead of where the fireworks would go off into the star-lit night sky above us. We were surrounded by couples, large groups of teenagers, families with young children, some obvious tourists and backpackers—most with cameras of various sizes in their hands and bottles of alcohol, waiting for it to hit midnight. At about twenty to midnight, I received a call from my mother telling me that they had finally arrived at our designated meeting point.

"Baby, it's only twenty minutes till the celebrations start. Are you sure you want to go look for them now?" my boyfriend asked with reference to my family. "The three of them are together, so it should be okay. Let them enjoy it from where they are."

"Yes babe, but I already told Ammu I will go and meet them to bring them here. They will get a much better view of the fireworks from here than where they are at the moment. I will be back before the fireworks start."

"Trust me, it will be impossible," he said, adding after a short pause, "Besides it will be nice if it's just the two of us, you know."

I knew then what he was thinking the entire time but failed to tell me out loud. The determined tone in his voice was a give-away, regardless of how he phrased it. He had wanted to celebrate the night just with me right from the start. I didn't want the New Year's Eve to turn out like my birthday, so I called and confirmed that it was okay with my family. They understood, knowing how thick the crowd was by now and that time was of the essence.

As the clock hit midnight, the entire sky was illuminated with a spectacular fireworks' display. Blue, green, purple, red, white, and a mixture of various other colours brightened up the city skyline. They were as bright as they were loud. For many Melbournians this was a New Year's Eve tradition which never got boring. For all the tourists flocking to the city from the northern hemisphere to take advantage of the warmer weather, this was much more attractive than standing out in the cold to celebrate the night. Thousands of screaming voices wished each other a prosperous year ahead. Cheers and laughter were in abundance as were warm embraces. With the brilliant display of fireworks within our sight, when my partner and I locked our lips into a passionate tender kiss, I had long forgotten about my New Year plans in Paris underneath the Eiffel Tower.

A marvellous start to the year! I had always felt truly blessed to have such a wonderful family, and to be surrounded by some amazing friends. This year I was feeling exceptionally blessed to have met that special someone who cared about me as much as I cared about him. A few minor glitches on New Year's Eve did not dampen my mood. I was still on cloud nine as the New Year began to take shape.

On one hot summer's day into the first week of the New Year, both my boyfriend and I had the day off work. University was still out which meant we had the entire day to ourselves, so we decided to head to the beach. He arrived to pick me up from my house around noon. As we were driving towards Williamstown beach, about twenty-five minutes to the south-west of where I lived, I noticed he was rather quiet. I could barely get two words out of him during the ride. He was not exactly the most talkative guy, unless he was super-excited about something special, but this was unusual even for him. I knew something was bothering him.

"Sweetie, I know something is bothering you. Do you want to talk about it?" I enquired.

"No, it's nothing. I am just a little tired." I knew it was not 'nothing', and I had also come to learn by now that if there was something bothering him, he needed to be probed.

"Come on, baby. Whatever it is, you know you can talk to me about it, right? I am always happy to listen."

"Yeah, I know." pausing for a minute he continued. "Well, it's my parents."

"What about them? Are they OK?" I asked, my tone sympathetic.

"They are having some problems."

"What kind of problems?" I asked almost expecting it to be either health-related or financial.

"I did not tell you this before, but my parents have always had marital issues while I was growing up. I thought it was all resolved now, but it looks like the problems may have re-surfaced."

"Sorry, I had no idea." I replied, not knowing what else to say at this point.

"My parents never saw eye-to-eye on how their children should be raised. They were always both too busy with their work. Both ran their own companies. It was unsaid, but I felt they were always competing against each other: who made more money, whose business was more successful, who could buy the better gifts for us on special occasions. It all revolved around money. They weren't really ever there for us.

Never there for support and guidance. It led to my siblings and I doing some rather stupid things as teenagers. To rebel out against them. That led to more problems. It was this vicious cycle that I didn't know how to unwind."

"I'm so sorry, darling. You were just a kid. I'm not surprised you felt like you needed to act out."

"At one point, things got so out of hand that I demanded my parents send me to Australia. I told them I would ask to be emancipated if they didn't, which left them no choice."

"You made a life for yourself here. You have turned a new leaf. I am sure they appreciate that."

"I thought if I was out of the picture, it would help them mend their relationship. I would stay out of sight. There would be no more trouble. I hoped it would help me get some peace of mind too. I won't have to hear or see them fight every night. I just couldn't take it anymore, you know?"

"Did it help their relationship?"

"Well, the first time I went to visit them after being in Australia for a year, I had never seen them happier. They were getting along so well. They were so happy to have me there for the holidays. It was a perfect vacation."

He paused to take a deep breath and then continued.

"A few days after I left Bangladesh following that trip, my aunt told me it was all an act. They pretended to be happy so I could be fooled. They didn't want to cause any concern. Apparently things took a turn for the worse after I left. They never wanted to get a divorce or be separated, being too scared of what other people might say. They love the façade. Now I hear they are not even talking to each other. About anything. It's like they are housemates, only they hate each other."

"Have you tried to talk to them?" I asked.

"What's the point? This is what I have known all my life. This is how I grew up—in a broken family. I know things will never change."

"Baby, it's worth a shot. You want to see your parents happy, don't you?"

"I do."

"Then, talk to them. Talk to each of them separately. Figure out what exactly is going on. Find out what is the latest that drove them to this point. Tell them how you feel."

"What if it doesn't do any good?"

"If not for anything else, you owe it to yourself to give it a try. What have you got to lose?"

"I suppose so."

"When we get back home tonight, you are going to call them. OK? I will be right by your side."

"Thank you, baby. I really appreciate it."

"Anytime. You know I'm always here for you."

"I do."

He then suddenly pulled up the car on the side of the road, put it in park gear, and leaned forward towards me. Giving me a tender kiss he uttered something that totally caught me by surprise.

"I love you," he muttered.

Without even thinking about whether or not I was ready to say those words back to him, I found myself responding with the same. I always considered myself to be a romantic at heart, but had never said it to anyone I had dated before. I didn't say what I didn't believe in, and I wasn't sure if I had truly loved them. But this was different. Everything with him felt different. Much more intense, much more fun, much more complicated, much more dramatic, much more romantic. I knew I had finally fallen. We had fallen. We were in love.

Chapter 9

*F*ebruary 14th, Valentine's Day. I had been waiting for this day forever. I was waiting for the day when I would celebrate it with someone I was truly in love with. This was going to be that year, my year.

Both my partner and I took the day off work to ensure nothing got in the way of us celebrating. We decided the day would be mine to organise and the night his. I told him I was going to come over to his house around one in the afternoon. I knew he would be sleeping in until noon, so I knew he would not have a clue as to what I had planned. Instead of heading over to his house at one as I told him, I decided to give him a surprise by going over there at eleven in the morning. I would cook him breakfast.

Sharp at eleven in the morning, I arrived with all the ingredients I would need to serve up a storm. I had bought some pancake mix, milk, eggs, maple syrup, oranges, strawberries and chocolates. On the menu were freshly-squeezed orange juice, scrambled eggs and pancakes with a side of strawberries dipped in chocolate. What could be better than a hearty breakfast to start off one's day?

As expected, I was welcomed by a sleepy boy at the door wearing only his shorts. The smile on his face as he saw me enter was exactly what I was hoping for. I greeted him cheerily and asked him to get back to bed until I called for him. After half an hour of preparing the food, I laid everything out on the dining table. He got up, brushed his teeth, and joined me.

"Oh my goodness! Look at all these!" he exclaimed. "Were you planning this all along?"

"Of course!"

"You know that's why I love you," he responded giving me a kiss.

"Come on! Let's eat while everything is still hot." I ushered him to sit down as I served three pancakes on his plate.

The breakfast was decadent. He thoroughly enjoyed everything I had prepared, and was touched at the gesture. I was very content that it was all so appetising. We both filled ourselves with a healthy serving of each—pancakes, eggs, strawberries with chocolate, and freshly squeezed orange juice to drink. After we finished our breakfast and put the dishes away, I relayed the plan for the rest of the day to him.

"I thought after breakfast we should go to the park given how wonderful the weather is today. I have actually packed a picnic for lunch. The basket is in my car."

"Sounds amazing!" he exclaimed. "I just need to have a quick shower first and get changed."

After he showered, and changed into a pair of jeans and a light-grey T-shirt, we headed out in my car. The temperature was in the low-thirties and a tad humid. Once in the park, we found ourselves a spot underneath a large oak tree to stay away from the direct glare of the sun. He laid out the picnic rug onto the ground, and I put down the lunch basket on top of it in one corner. We both took off our shoes and made ourselves comfortable on the rug. He then pulled me close, looked me in the eyes and gently tugged away the few strands of my dark hair covering my face behind the ears. Using both hands to cup my face, he first kissed me on my left cheek and then the right. Slowly he moved his mouth towards mine and pecked on my upper lip. We locked our lips in an intense kiss. I held my breath. He slowly slid his hands down the back of my neck and rested them on my spine. I clutched his strong arms with my hands. Before we knew it we were lying on the rug, my body on top of his, our lips still locked in a kiss; his arms pulling me closer to him, my arms clutching his biceps, and our legs intertwined. Every now and then, he would unlock from the kiss to caress my neck and ears with his lips. Being completely in the moment, we rolled around on the rug a couple of times until I reminded him softly that there were people around.

"You aren't embarrassed, are you?" he asked.

"May be just a little shy." I whispered into his ear.

He smiled, responded with a strong last kiss before sitting up straight to iron out his T-shirt. We sat on the rug quietly for a few moments, taking in the view of our surroundings. The park was lush green, and the flower-beds were colourful with pink, purple, blue, orange—flowers of all different varieties. The air was fresh and crisp, with a festive feel to it. After about half an hour of idle chit chat, we opened the picnic basket and dug into our lunch. We took our time relishing it slowly while watching other couples in the park celebrating Valentine's Day, or those walking their dogs or taking advantage of the sun, tanning. Once we were done, I drove him back to his house and said goodbye. I drove myself home, looking forward to finding out what he had planned for us that evening.

I had bought a new dress to wear on our date. I wanted to look stunning and blow him away when he came to pick me up for dinner. I started getting ready almost as soon as I arrived home—there was always so much to do if you wanted to look perfect. After a scrub and a bath, I painted my nails a seductive shade of rose. Even though my shoulder-length hair was naturally straight, I used my VS Sassoon straightener to give it a lift using some styling gel to hold it in place. The straightener was a gift from work for being a 'high-performer'. I liked how using it boosted the caramel highlights I had tinted my hair with. After my nails dried, I put on my make-up—foundation, bronzer, mascara, eye liner, eye-shadow, lip gloss—the whole nine yards. Everything I wore was to make sure it complemented my dress, through contrasting colours, which I put on next. It was a beautiful white satin dress with minor black prints. The dress stood out against my light brown skin, caressing my slim five-foot-seven hourglass figure up to the knees. I put the bare necessities in a small black clutch hand-bag including a tiny mirror and the lip-gloss I was wearing, before pulling out my shoes from the wardrobe. It was a pair of black Steve Madden heels to match my handbag and the prints on my dress. I put everything down, including the wrapped Valentine's Day gift for my boy, next to my bedroom door so I could grab them and leave as soon as he arrived to pick me up.

My partner arrived sharp at seven. Just as I received his missed call on my mobile, I grabbed everything I had pre-organised to take with me, said goodbye to my mother and ran out the door. As I took my seat next to him in the car, I leaned over for a kiss as he told me he thought I looked gorgeous. He looked devastatingly handsome himself in a full-sleeved black silk shirt and a pair of black trousers with his short hair styled to give it the 'wet-look'.

"You don't look so bad yourself", I returned the compliment.

"We make one striking couple!" He said with a cheeky smile on his face, and drove out of my driveway.

We drove to Chapel Street in Prahran, one of the many suburbs in Melbourne popular for its exquisite culinary culture. As we were seated at our table when we arrived at the restaurant and after we had ordered, I reached into the bag I was carrying that contained my gift for him. I handed it to him from across the table. He took it with a beaming smile and ripped open the wrapping paper like an impatient child on Christmas morning. The genuine stunned look on his face as he opened the box was priceless.

"Oh my gosh! Baby, what have you done?" he asked as he stared at the TAG Heuer watch that lay in the box. "Why did you get this for me? It must have cost you a fortune!"

"Well, I knew you really wanted it so I had been saving up for it. I really wanted to get this for you." I explained. I knew how he loved owning things with reputable brand names and had learnt a while ago that there was a certain watch he had his eye on.

"I don't know what to say!" he exclaimed once more. "Thank you so much."

"Happy Valentine's Day."

"Happy Valentine's Day," he repeated after me with a kiss.

Our entrée arrived right then. I could not tell if he had a gift for me too so I presumed the dinner was his gift, given it was an expensive one for a student working part-time. The both of us tremendously enjoyed the soups we had ordered for entrée, the grilled salmon with a side of salad I had ordered for main and he the rib-eye steak. I was in the mood for something sweet, so to finish off I ordered a sticky date pudding with a serve of vanilla ice cream and caramel sauce. He wasn't as much into desserts as I was, so he only had a couple of spoonfuls of my pudding. He settled the bill at the end of the meal and I thanked my valentine for a lovely dinner. He drove me back to my house and asked if he could come in for a cup of coffee before having to drive back all the way home.

I brewed some fresh coffee and poured it into two cups. He was sitting on my bed as I took the cups into the bedroom and passed one to him. As I sat down across from him on the bed and started to sip my steaming cup of coffee, he said,

"I have a little something for you."

"You already bought me dinner. I thought that was the gift!"

I was trying to be polite but still very eager to find out what he got for me. After all, who didn't like presents?

"There is something else. Here, give me your coffee."

He took the cup from my hand and put it on the bedside table. Then he got out a small box covered in royal blue velvet from the left pocket of his trousers. He opened it and took out a small piece of jewellery. I could not see what it was as his big hands covered it from my view. Before I had a chance to realise what was happening, he grabbed by left hand and slipped the jewellery on my ring finger.

"Baby, this is my present to you. It's a promise ring. I promise to love you forever, and when we are both ready, buy you an even bigger ring. I know we have only known each other for a few months but I know there is no one else I want to spend the rest of my life with. I know there is no other 'one' for me. Only you. I love you."

My mouth dropped wide open in astonishment. Both his action and his words took me by total surprise. It was so sudden, so unexpected. I didn't know how to respond or act. I stared at the ring on my finger for a few minutes. The room was so quiet you could hear even a pin drop. He squeezed my hand to snap me out of my daze. Still in utter shock I mumbled "I love you too" and kissed his soft lips.

Chapter 10

*E*ver since I was a little girl, I had believed birthdays were special. Given it was the day that someone was born, I believed it was the perfect opportunity to show them how much their presence in your life meant to you. I knew that not everyone saw it the same way; therefore I did not expect them to celebrate mine as I would theirs. Nonetheless, I always got excited when the birthday for someone I cared about came around. I would start thinking about what gifts to get for them months in advance, and what I could do to make them feel as special as they really were to me. Until now I had been taking a lot of pleasure in organising the day for my family members on their birthdays, or contributing to those of my friends. Granted the surprise party I had thrown for Sumara on her eighteenth had been a total bust, but normally they always brought joy to my family. Now it was turn for the man I loved. I was more excited than I had ever been before.

I remember my partner telling me once when we first started dating that his point of view on birthdays was a little different to mine, especially when it came to that of his own. He didn't have the best memories of his birthdays until now, and therefore, didn't like to make a fuss over it. Birthdays had not been as much of an occasion to celebrate at his household as they were in mine. Some had been smeared with family disputes, others almost non-existent. He told me that the year before he did absolutely nothing to commemorate the day. So I needed to show him this year why it didn't need to be that way. I was determined to give him a pleasant memory of the day, hoping to erase all the awful ones of the past, and possibly one that he would never forget.

My first course of action was to call his housemate, and ask if I could have the house to myself on the evening of his birthday. He agreed, adding he would leave the spare set of keys for me underneath a pot of plant on the front porch. My partner wanted to go to work that evening, so I didn't say 'no'. It would give me an opportunity to set things up at the house while he was away. I started preparing some of the items for dinner at my house during the day because he didn't leave for work until later in the afternoon. I had marinated a whole chicken overnight with soy sauce and various spices to make sure the flavour infused and the meat remained tender when it was barbecued. I placed it on the grill at my house so I would only need to heat it up before serving at his. Even though the chicken would have been more than enough for the two us, I also barbecued a large T-bone steak, his favourite, which I had also marinated overnight. I didn't prepare a steak for myself—I was more into chicken than beef.

While the meat was on the grill in the backyard, I prepared the dough to bake him a birthday cake. Normally I wasn't much into baking except for the occasional cupcakes or muffins. So to make sure the cake tasted delicious, I decided to download a recipe off the internet and follow it to the letter. When the dough was ready, I poured it into the pan and shoved it in the oven. I rushed back to check the meat, and then back again to check the cake. After a few times of rushing back and forth to make sure I didn't burn anything, finally it was time to get the meat off the grill. Once the meat was done, I placed some slices of potatoes, capsicums and onions on the barbecue, the taste of which I loved grilled. By then the cake was almost ready so I prepared the icing. As I switched off the oven, and waited for the cake to cool a little before adding the icing, I went back to check the vegetables. They were done too except for the slices of potatoes. I put the capsicums and onions onto a plate, then went back into the kitchen to finish icing the cake. Ten minutes later, my rich chocolate mud cake with creamy chocolate icing was ready to be enjoyed. Putting it aside on the kitchen bench-top, I went back outside to get the potatoes off the grill, switch the grill off and then head inside with the fruits of my labour. Once in the kitchen, I put everything into multiple pots that I could easily carry in the car with me while driving to his house. I placed the cake carefully on a tray and covered it with a plastic lid, using foil to wrap around it, so it didn't move much while in the car. I also took the frozen Sarah Lee sticky date pudding I had bought the day before, from the freezer, and placed it in a bag. By now, he had gotten addicted to my favourite dessert and we loved sharing a few slices of sticky date pudding after a special meal.

I changed into my jeans and a top before placing all the food items in the car. I placed them on the passenger's seat at the front so I could keep an eye during the hour-long drive. I threw the bag containing the dress and the shoes I was going to wear that night at the back before getting in the car. As I drove, in my head I began to tick off a mental list to make sure I hadn't forgotten anything—food, desserts, clothes, shoes, candles . . . Oops! I realised I had forgotten his present! I turned around. I had only been driving for ten minutes, so I was glad I didn't remember it any later than that. I rushed into my room, grabbed his gift from the cupboard and ran back outside. Now I had everything I needed for a birthday dinner he would never forget.

After an hour and a quarter, I reached my destination. I found the keys under the pot on the front porch as I had expected. I grabbed it, opened the front door, checked to make sure the house was empty, and then set out to get things organised. All I needed to do was make sure the food was kept warm, prepare the salad, and set the table. I put the meat in the oven without switching it on, and placed the rest of the items on the kitchen bench-top. Getting together the chopping board, a knife, and the ingredients for the Greek Salad I was about to make, I started to chop away. Once that was done, I grabbed the place-mats, plates, glasses and cutleries to set the table. When I was satisfied with how the table looked, I ducked into his bedroom to get changed. I slipped into the dress I had brought with me—a grey cotton dress that hugged my figure, and the matching pair of flats. I lightly freshened up my make-up and waited for him to get home. As I waited, I placed candles in the dining room, the living room and the bedroom. The candles on the cake were lit last. When I heard the engine of his car as he pulled into the drive-way, I switched off all the lights in the house. I took the well-lit cake and stood with it near the doorway. The keys turned in the lock at the front door, and a stunned face peeked inside.

"Happy Birthday, my love!" I whispered.

"Oh my goodness!" he said placing his right hand on his heart. "You totally caught me by surprise."

I said smiling at him "Didn't mean to startle you. Sorry!"

"It's fine baby. It *is* a lovely surprise." He leaned forward and kissed me.

"Make a wish."

He blew out the candles and murmured something under his breath. He put his left arm around my waist as we walked back together into the living room. I placed the cake in one corner of the dining table. The place-settings were already on the table, indicating a romantic dinner for two, accompanied by a couple of candles at each end and a small vase of tulips in the centre. The chicken and the steak lay on their respective platters decorated with the grilled vegetables, and the salad in a bowl. I had cut some slices of Vienna bread as well, and presented it with some sun-dried tomatoes. A bottle of apple cider was going to be our substitute for wine.

"This is amazing!" he exclaimed admiring what lay on the table. "I love you!"

"Are you hungry?" I asked, excited with his reaction.

"Yes, but the hunger is just going to have to wait a little longer. I need to thank someone first for her efforts."

He took my hand and pulled me towards him. Lifting me off the ground, he carried me into the bedroom and laid me down on the bed. Gently placing his body on top of mine, he kissed me on my neck and my cheeks. He removed the dress off my shoulders to caress them with his lips. Then he slowly moved up again until he found my mouth. His hands were behind my head, pulling my face towards his. Mine moved across over his shoulders, before finally finding their place under his shirt on his bare back. The kiss was intense. I could feel every bone of his body as he pressed against me. I could hardly breathe. As we continued to kiss, he slipped his hands under my dress, and pulled it across over my belly. Then slowly he moved his mouth away from mine and placed them on my tummy as he started to kiss it. He only stopped when I started to gasp for breath. Caressing my body, he gave one last kiss before we headed back to the dinner that awaited us.

At the dinner table, he served me a portion of the chicken and some vegetables. He put the steak from the platter onto his plate. I grabbed a couple of slices of bread and passed on the plate to him. He helped himself to some, and then poured some gravy on top of his steak. I poured the apple cider into two wine glasses and handed him one. Looking into each other's eyes, we said "Cheers" and clicked our glasses together before taking a sip. We talked about how our day was while we digged into the food. Everything tasted amazing, especially given how hungry we both were. Once he had finished with his steak, he cut himself a small portion of the chicken to get a taste of it. I served us both some more salad. When we were done with the main course, I took the used plates from the table and dropped them into the kitchen sink. Placing two clean plates onto the table, I brought out the sticky-date pudding with a large serving of vanilla ice cream on the side and two slices of the home-baked chocolate mud cake. By the time we finished our dessert, we could barely move. After resting for a few minutes, my partner stood up and headed towards the living room. I walked into his bedroom to grab his birthday gift from the bag that I had been hiding it in. As he sat himself down on the couch in the living room, I walked in with the wrapped present.

"There is still more?" he asked, astonished.

"Just a little something." I said, handing it over to him. "Open it."

As he tore open the wrapping paper, he found two envelops—one contained a card and the other the gift. He first opened the envelop with the card in it, read the note on the card, kissed me on the forehead, and then opened the other envelop. As it ripped open, he gasped.

"No you didn't!"

"I hope you like it," I murmured softly.

"Like it? I love it!" he shouted. "You can't keep spoiling me like this, baby."

"Only because I love you. Besides, these are as much for me as are for you."

I smiled. I was going to enjoy this gift too, but I knew how much he would love it. This was his passion—cars. I was into cars as well, but he was downright devoted. He was a car fanatic, and this was the ultimate gift for a twenty-something year old male who loved cars and races. He was holding in his hands the tickets to the Melbourne Formula One Grand Prix for that season. It would be the first time that either of us enjoyed the event live. I was looking forward to sharing in his passion. As we prepared to build our life together, this was a gesture to let him know I was ready to be a part of everything that was important to him. And in return all I wished for was that he reciprocated the same.

Chapter 11

As I reluctantly dragged myself out of bed on the second day as a single lady for the first time in five years, I wondered how I was going to get through another day of 'faking' it. It was still a work-day which meant pretending the day was like any other—get ready, get breakfast and get myself out the door. I considered calling in sick but I realised what I really needed was to be distracted, surrounded by people who didn't know much about my personal life and would not pity me on the tragic turn my relationship had taken. Come to think of it, I still had not told my family that I had called off the engagement. It was going to take me all the strength I had to break the news to my mother, and I just could not muster enough of it right then. The fact that my partner, or my ex-partner, had not called me since two nights ago ran briefly through my mind but I shoved it aside, convincing myself it was a good thing. It was not a lot of surprise that he hadn't tried to call again or just drop by—usually such events were a game to him and were always about the battle of power. There was a time when I wished, naively enough, that such games would stop after we got engaged. I had always considered them to be immature and child-like but sometimes had succumbed to them to avoid turning out to be the weaker link. This break up, furthermore, did still have the potential to end up like the many others we tried during our five-year-long courtship. So distance was exactly what I needed to stay determined.

The first half of the day was a blur—meetings, coffee-breaks, a failed attempt to complete a dashboard report, and being finally saved by the invitation to join some friends of mine for lunch as soon as it hit mid-day. These were friends I had met through various events at the company where I was working, most being of similar age to myself. Almost all of them had started to work at the company that same year, which meant it was still a blooming friendship. As I had only been acquainted with them for less than a couple of months, they had still not met my ex-partner but heard that there was a man in my life. I had been hanging out a lot with my new-found friends, which right now was a much better prospect than being around my best friends from university. I was not looking forward to breaking the news of my decision to my best friends. I did not believe they would totally support me on this. They might suggest it's a rash decision, a case of the cold feet. They would try to convince me to take some time to think it through. They had known my ex-partner since a few months after we had started dating, found him handsome and charming, and thought of him as an extension of myself. They would convince me to get back together and stop being foolish. That was because they did not know the whole truth about our relationship. I never liked dishing out the dirty laundry, so they only knew about all the good times we have had and pictured us as the perfect couple. They knew absolutely nothing of the abuse, which I was too ashamed to share with *anyone*, close or not.

My company office, like most others in Melbourne, was on Collins Street in the Central Business District (CBD). We decided to meet for lunch at "Australia on Collins", a stone's throw away from our office and a haven for city-shoppers with over sixty specialty stores, alongside a large food-court catering to all professionals working in the CBD. We found ourselves at the usual meeting place right outside the front entrance around ten past the hour. By the time everyone had gathered, there were about fifteen of us hungry for lunch and ready to engage in some idle office gossip. As we entered the food-court, and with much difficulty found a couple of tables next to each other to sit the whole group, we decided to break out in different directions to buy what we wanted to eat and meet back at the tables. After walking past the couple of Asian stalls, and the Middle-Eastern kebab shop, I landed in front of the Italian stall and ordered myself a serving of gnocchi with my usual drink, a bottle of diet coke. Grabbing some serviettes and cutlery as well on the way out, I headed towards the tables we had reserved for our large crowd. As I approached the tables, I put everything down on one of them and with my freed-up hands, pulled one of the chairs toward me to sit down on. The moment I did so, one of the boys from my group of friends pulled it back away from me and said in a mocking voice,

"You can't sit here!"

It was a normal behaviour for him, and I should not have been the least bit surprised. Some of the boys there often acted like they were still in high-school, rather *primary* school, often teasing us girls randomly trying to get under our skin. No outsider would believe we were a bunch of professionals working for one of the biggest multinational corporations in Australia. For some reason, many of them found pleasure in making me their target, which I assumed was because of my reactions to their immaturity. They found it amusing. If this was any other day, the usual reaction for me would be to say something back to tease him in return, and pull the chair back to myself. There would have been at least two more minutes of each of us pulling the chair away from the other until either he gave up or I gave in and sat down somewhere else. It would all have been in fun and games, without anyone getting hurt. But not today.

Before I knew it, as soon as he said those words, I could feel tears forming at the corners of my eyes. I could not allow my colleagues to see that I was about to break down and cry over a minor case of friendly teasing. I immediately grabbed my food and drink off the table, said a hasty goodbye and ran out the food court as fast as I could. As I walked around like a crazy girl looking desperately for the ladies' washrooms, the teardrops began to fall. After a couple of minutes of frantic search, I located the toilets on the ground floor of the shopping centre. Finally, as soon as I locked myself behind the safety of one of the stalls in the washrooms, there was no holding back. What started out as sobbing soon turned into a full-blown cry, as I thrust myself into a corner. I cried uncontrollably for at least fifteen minutes. I could not believe the reaction I was having to the playful teasing I had gotten so used to by now. I had reached breaking-point and could not take anymore. Holding it all back in since the night things fell apart finally had its repercussions. I cried like a child. I cried my heart out for the empty feeling inside of me, like my world had fallen apart, like everything I knew was taken away from me. I cried at the thought of feeling lonely, not being able to talk to him, no longer receiving his daily text messages, not being able to see him at the end of each day—sharing with him every minute detail of what had happened on that day—interesting or not, rushing to him whenever I had exciting news to share, or even comfort him when he was going through one of his depressive episodes. I cried because I was scared of the changes that were ahead of me, not being sure how I was going to live my life alone. These reasons had run through my mind time and time again when I was considering breaking up with him, reasons that stopped me from taking actions much sooner. Finally, I had decided it was better to feel this pain than the pain he was causing me. They say it gets better with time. I was wondering when that time would come.

I finally had to pull myself together, wipe my face and come out of the washroom. Reality was calling. I needed to get back to work. As I stepped outside I was relieved that no one had followed me as I ran out on lunch. All I wanted to do was head back to the office, block my mind of every thought of him and hope I had the strength to hold it back until I was in the safe haven of my room later that day. I took a deep breath and prayed that there would be no repetition of the events of that afternoon. I knew the situation was made more difficult by the fact that I was not discussing it with anyone, but it would be a while until I was ready to. For so many years I had only bared my soul to one person that to have the role replaced would be no easy task. He preferred to keep our private matters private, and I respected that, so for me it was not like other twenty-something girls whose relationship details were discussed within friend circles. I was more like what I had watched my mother and aunts to be like, as I knew how important that would be if this person was going to be my husband. If he was going to be respected as my partner by my friends and family, I needed to keep certain things under wraps. Even though none of those mattered any more, I was still very conscious of my poor judgements. I needed time.

After an entire week of not seeing her son-in-law-to-be around in the house, my mother finally got suspicious. That weekend she asked me if we had a fight. My first instinct was just to say 'yes' and keep on doing what I was, but I realised it was about time. The sooner I did it, the more real it would become. The more chance it would have of withstanding any sudden urge I may have had to run back to what I had left behind. I pulled up a chair at our dining room table and asked my mother to take a seat.

"Ammu, there is something I need to tell you." I opened my mouth, not being quite sure on how to phrase it.

Taking a deep breath, I continued, "I broke up with him."

She had a stunned look on her face. "When?"

"Last weekend. Sorry it took me so long to tell you. No one else knows yet and I don't know how to talk about it."

"What happened?" she asked gently, placing her right hand on my shoulder.

"Everything. You know how we have been having problems since the engagement. Well honestly, even before that. I finally realised I did not want to marry someone who did not respect me, you or my family enough. I know how difficult it is for people to change, and I finally realised that he would never change. *We* would never change. I don't want to be constantly fighting with my partner, and I don't want to see my partner fighting with my mum or my sisters. I don't want to have to constantly explain myself or my family to him, or apologise for who we are. That's not how I want to spend the rest of my life. I want everyone to just get along. I have tried long enough. We are just not good for each other."

I explained as best as I could but left out the number one reason for the break-up. I was not going to feel like the victim. I did not want her pity. I knew I had made the choice that was right for me.

"Ammu, I would rather make this decision now and call off the engagement than just bear it for the rest of my life. It is better than getting a divorce, right?"

"Are you sure this is what you want?" she interjected. "Are you sure this is not a hasty decision, a heat-of-the-moment thing because you were angry at each other?"

"I have been thinking about it for over six months and I finally had the guts to do it. Yes, I am sure."

"Okay then, I will stand by you one hundred percent."

I then realised the reason why my mother would not need more convincing than that. Apart from knowing me well enough, that when I was determined there was no changing my mind, she was also a lot more aware of the true nature of our relationship than my friends. This was not because I would discuss with her or my family what happened behind closed doors. Given he was around in the house as much as he was, my family was witness to the events that happened there. He was a part of all family gatherings because my mother wanted him to feel like he had a family in Melbourne he could call his own. On the downside, it meant he also unwillingly became a player in the scuffles, or at the least a witness, normal to any family. I could not shelter him from those as I could not shelter my family from his and mine.

"Thank you. I really need your support on this right now." I replied to my mother before I started to voice my true concerns about the break-up.

"What are you going to tell our relatives? I know it is not going to be easy for you. Lucky we don't live in Bangladesh otherwise it would have only been that much harder. Oh, or even worse, all your friends here who had attended the engagement party? I am so sorry, Mum. I would prefer if you didn't mention it to anyone right away. I am just not ready to play twenty questions."

"Don't worry about that. I won't discuss it with any one willingly, but when people start to wonder I will just mention that things did not work out. I don't need to provide any explanation."

I always had a lot of respect for my mother on how she handled prying relatives or family friends. For months before calling off the engagement, I continuously wondered if by doing this I would bring shame upon her. Let alone having to deal with all the relatives who would have a thousand questions to understand what went wrong, the same situation would arise while trying to deal with those within the Bangladeshi community in Melbourne. It's not that everyone had poor intention—some would be genuinely concerned. However my experience to date had taught me that that number would be relatively small. For most others, it would be another scandal they could gossip about at community gatherings and tea-parties. I could see the hook into their story—the perfect daughters not so perfect after all. Unfortunately in such situations, where breaking up of engagements or divorces were concerned, I knew quite well that almost one hundred percent of the time it would just be assumed it was the girl's fault. She either didn't know how to compromise, or adjust, or had some quality missing in her that led to the demise of the relationship. It was hardly ever the fault of the boy. As much as I hated to admit it, I had let all these scare me away from doing what was right for a very long time.

Luckily for me dealing with controversies was made easier by the fact that I was not living in Bangladesh. If I was, the inquisition would have been a hundred times worse. Now, it was something that my mother would still have to deal with but over the phone, rather than being in the midst of it all. With regards to those Bangladeshis here—well, I pretty much decided from the very first day that I would stop attending any functions or parties organised by any members of the community. If I happened to bump into anyone on the streets, which was luckily a rare occasion, I could handle it. But it would be a very long time until I would be ready to face their judging looks in a large get-together. I knew then that I would also stay away from my own house the first few times my mother invited over her friends for dinners or to celebrate special occasions like Eid. I was going to be a coward but I would rather she dealt with all that right now than I. *I* still had to tell my sisters . . . and my best friends.

Chapter 12

It was a Wednesday night, almost a week and half after the break-up. After another tiring and stressful day at work, I finally arrived home, had my dinner with the family and tucked myself away in my room. As I looked through the window, I saw how dark it was outside. I could barely make out the raindrops sliding against the window and hear them against the slant of the roof. Stooping over on my bed, my legs covered by a thin blanket, I was soothed by the soft sound of the rain. I picked up my mobile, from the top of the bedside table, next to the lamp that Romana had bought for me on my previous birthday. I started writing a text message.

"Hi girls. It's me! I was hoping we can do brunch this Sunday somewhere in St. Kilda. I've something I really want 2 talk to u about. Hope u are all free! Let me know where u want to meet . . . xoxo"

I selected three names from the contact list—Ashleigh, Jema and Nilie—and pressed the 'send' button. In about ten seconds I received three synonymous "yes". Nilie, as I had hoped, also suggested that we go to the restaurant Stokehouse for brunch. We all planned to meet at the Luna Park car park around noon and walk together to the restaurant from there.

Just before mid-day on Sunday, as I drove from my house to St. Kilda, our favourite suburb by the beach for brunches, I thought of how I was going to break the news to my best friends. After a lot of thinking, I decided I had procrastinated about this for long enough. Now that I had finally taken the step to tell them, I would just play it by ear and stay strong.

Finally at about quarter past twelve, I saw the three girls getting out of Nilie's car. They approached me at the entrance of the Luna Park car park. We greeted each other with the usual kiss on the cheeks. Nilie advised that she had made a 12 o'clock reservation for us at Stokehouse, so we needed to walk rather quickly or jog there, if we intended to make it. The restaurant was quite popular amongst Melbournians and a reservation was usually necessary. We didn't want to get the reservation cancelled or have to wait in line at another restaurant, so we walked as fast as our legs could carry us. It was a beautiful sunny day which meant more than the usual number of brunch-goers hunting for restaurants in St Kilda. As soon as we arrived at the restaurant, we asked to be seated in the terrace upstairs over-looking the beach. Once upstairs, I also pointed towards what looked like to be the quietest table possible in the crowded restaurant. I had not requested Nilie to suggest a quiet little restaurant or a café for our impromptus gathering, unwilling to raise an alarm. I just wanted to break the news as calmly and normally as I possibly could.

Once seated, everyone looked at me inquisitively wondering why they had all been summoned. Without keeping them in suspense for much longer, I broke the news. It was followed by an explanation of why I believed it was the right decision for me. I found myself listing many of the reasons but still could not bear to discuss what ultimately had kicked in and pushed me over the edge. I couldn't talk about being physically or verbally abused. I was still too ashamed to admit that it had happened to me. I also found myself retracing the steps in my head of the events of the morning on the day I finally called it quits.

It was just two Sundays ago that I was meeting my girls for one of our regular Sunday brunches. Well, the brunches used to be more regular while we were at university. However now that we were all working full-time and two of us were in relationships, it had become more occasional than regular. Nonetheless, it was still a favourite pass-time of ours and we tried to do it as often as our busy schedules would allow us. That morning, as I was getting ready to meet with the girls, my then fiancé was getting ready to head to work.

"Where are you headed?" he asked as he saw me changing out of my pyjamas.

"I am meeting with the girls for a catch up. Can't believe it has almost been a month since we all saw each other last." I replied.

"I don't like you hanging out with your friends so much," he said bluntly.

"I just said I haven't seen them for almost a month!"
The tone in my voice gave away that he could soon be
testing my patience.

"We are engaged now. You are soon to be my wife. I
don't like you going out so much," he said in a sharp
controlled voice.

My instincts told me he was still fuming over the incident
of the night before. He was using my laptop to do some
work that night and came across some photos of myself
with my colleagues. They were taken a couple of weeks
ago at a work-event. It was a costume party so I was
dressed up as Marie Antoinette. I posed for the camera
when the photo was taken as I was being handed the
award for 'best-dressed'. Next to me was one of my male
colleagues who decided it would be funny to try to ruin
the photo by jumping into it as the flash went on. It was
innocent, all very innocent. Even I was taken by surprise
when the colleague jumped into the picture. However, in
my partner's eyes it was insulting for him if I was seen
with another man in a photo. It didn't matter what the
context was. To him it was bringing him and his family
down—having his fiancée take a photo with another
man. The whole thing was blown out of proportion and
we went to bed upset at one another.

"So . . . what, now that we are engaged you are always
going to tell me what I should do or should not do? How
often I should see my friends? It's not even like you are
here and I am leaving you to be with them—you are
going to work!"

"Well, I am telling you that I don't like it!" he countered, raising his voice a few notches higher.

"You want to control me all the time, is that it? I always need to ask your permission?" It was a rhetorical question. I sounded frustrated, but not as angry as something like this would normally make me.

"Yes, yes, yes. You have to ask my permission." He challenged, "What are you going to do about it?"

"Well, this is what I will do." I responded, deadly calm, sounding almost cold. I did the only thing I knew how to in order to avoid another argument getting out of hand. I shoved my make-up into my handbag, slipped on my shoes and slammed the door shut behind me.

At that point, little did I know that it would be the last time I would be leaving my fiancé's apartment. If I had known, I would have grabbed the clothes, the extra pairs of shoes and other amenities that I kept at his apartment just in case I needed them. As I was walking out of the apartment, I hoped he would see sense when he calmed down, and we could discuss things rationally. I was tired of voices being raised. By then, I had started to get better at leaving. I became less and less inclined to deal with similar situations over and over again. As I jumped into my car and drove away, I was not even surprised at myself for the lack of tears that would usually be the norm because I was either too angry or too upset at his actions. I just knew that I didn't care as much anymore. I had finally grown out of the drama.

Ashleigh snapped me out of my thoughts.

"Hey, honey. Care to share?" she asked politely.

"Just thinking."

Neither she, nor the others, forced me to explain. They just waited patiently while I gathered my thoughts, stabbing away at the meal with their forks. I re-initiated my monologue.

"He was starting to get more and more controlling every day. It was as though he was becoming a different person since we got engaged. He worried more about what other people might think, how we might be perceived, than the actual relationship. Who knows how much of it was real, or how much of it was in his head. But because he was always so focused on this image he wanted of us as a couple that the relationship started to get unbearable. I felt like a third person watching from the outside the turn my relationship was taking. I was losing the person I had fallen in love with. Everything I found compatible about us was beginning to disappear. Everything I respected in him was beginning to disappear. This was the only way."

"Oh sweetie." Ashleigh gasped. "I wish you had confided in us much sooner."

Jema and Nilie resonated her words.

"I wanted to, but couldn't. When we first started to get serious, we agreed to keep private matters private. I wanted to respect that. Ironic, isn't it?"

"You were doing what you thought was right." Jema comforted me.

"I always saw the two of you as the perfect couple . . ." Nilie mused.

"Now you know!" I had a bit of sarcasm in my voice, but smiled at her as I said it. "I don't know. May be we *were*. Sure didn't feel like that anymore."

"I remember telling you at the Melbourne University ball when you brought him as your date never to let go of him. I remember thinking what a perfect catch he was." Nilie reminisced.

"Yeah, that was the first we met him. I remember now. We were all in such awe at what a handsome couple you two made." Ashleigh said as she giggled.

"The tall, handsome guy in the black suit and me in my long dark blue gown." I added, giggling with Ashleigh.

Jema started to theorise. "We know you are not a superficial person. We know that was never the reason why you fell in love with him or stayed with him. But may be on the outset, that's what we saw when we looked at you two. We thought you were perfect because you looked perfect. May be."

"How are you coping?" Nilie asked curiously.

"Up and down. Up and down. I need to constantly keep myself occupied. Otherwise it's hard. They say it gets better with time, so I am just waiting for time to pass." I said as I laughed absent-mindedly.

"You know where we are whenever you need us." Jema added.

"Yes, sweetie. Any time." Nilie echoed.

"Babe…" Ashleigh looked into my eyes and held her gaze. "If you need to keep yourself busy, you call me. Okay?"

"Yep, okay." I smiled weakly.

I heard what they were saying and I knew they meant it. I wished I could truly get myself to listen. However, the truth was that I needed to do this on my own. I needed to find the inner self I had lost over the years. I was searching to bring back the confident happy-go-lucky girl I was before I met him. Over the five years, I had lost pieces of myself I was told every girl must lose to make a relationship successful. It was necessary in order to learn how to compromise. While I did that, I was inadvertently giving parts of myself away to him. I handed over my independence as I learned about co-existence. The truth was, in my heart of hearts, I knew I had lost more than my fiancé. Never mind that such a word didn't exist—if the girls were my best friends, the person I had really lost was my "bestest".

Chapter 13

*I*t was well after midnight when a phone call suddenly woke me up.

"Hello?" I asked in a tiny voice.

"Hi baby. Were you asleep?" It was my partner calling.

"Yes, babe. What's up?"

"I just received some bad news from home. I don't know what to do."

"What happened?"

"My dad had a heart attack."

"I am so sorry! Is he in the hospital?"

"Yes, he is. He is not doing too well."

I could hear the sadness in his voice even if he were on the other end of the telephone.

"Sweetheart, why don't you come over?"

"Are you sure?"

"Yes, definitely. Come over. Give me a missed call when you get here. I will come and open the door for you."

About ten minutes later, I received his missed call. I got out of bed, put my slippers on and opened the front door. He was standing at the door with a solemn look on his face. I gave him a hug and ushered him in. He followed me to the bedroom. We both squeezed in onto my single-sized bed and cuddled.

"How did it happen, baby?" I enquired, after making ourselves comfortable underneath the covers.

"I received a text message from my brother about an hour ago asking me to call him. When I called, they were already in the hospital. My mum and dad had not been talking for over a month. But today they got into some sort of an argument over a property that my mother wants to purchase. I didn't ask for details. Apparently they had a screaming match for about twenty minutes when my father complained he had a chest pain. He felt light-headed and couldn't breathe. For a minute my mum thought it was just anxiety, but was soon alarmed. They called an ambulance and took him to the hospital straight away. The doctor confirmed it was an attack. They are looking after him now."

"I hope he will be okay. I hope it's not too severe."

The topic was too close to home. My father had suffered two heart attacks in the past before a severe cardiac arrest claimed his life. I was too young to remember the attacks but remembered him being away from home for several weeks at a stretch, looking weak and dishevelled when he finally returned. Every time he returned home, the number of various types of medicine he had to take seemed to increase. Later, when I started to study Biology in school, I had a much better understanding of his conditions. I knew he had high blood pressure but didn't look after himself well enough. He loved food, all kinds of food. To him that was living. Being deprived of what he wanted to eat was torture. He would always say, "Enjoy it while you can". He wasn't an overweight human being. He looked well, but I knew better. He had high cholesterol, didn't eat the healthiest and hated to exercise. I requested my mother to cook our meals with less spice, less oil and in general, less fatty foods. I remembered since a few months before he had passed away, I was always taking the beef or the lamb dishes away from in front of him at the dinner table, including anything cooked with eggs. He loved his red meat. I tried to warn him but he would always say, "We will all die sooner or later. Let me enjoy life while I can." He had, however, just started to listen. He was always regular with his medication and felt fitter than ever. It was obviously not enough.

"I hope so too. I know I don't talk to him much, but he is still my dad you know," my boyfriend responded, pulling me out of my thoughts.

"Yeah, I know." I added, "You should talk to him soon, make sure he is okay. Let him know you need him to look after himself. I couldn't do enough for my dad, but you still have a chance."

"You always bring up your dad," he muttered under his breath. I heard him but chose to ignore the comment. Everything sounded like a competition to him, even when it concerned sick or dying family members.

"I get so surprised at the number of people I know who has had heart attacks. Not everyone has been lucky. Most I know are barely even fifty."

"What can I do for him when I am so far away from home?"

"You can talk to him on the phone and try to get him to listen. Make sure he does take care of himself and does what the doctor tells him to."

"It won't be enough."

"Do you want to go to Bangladesh for a visit?"

"I can't with uni and work. Plus the flights are so expensive. I can't afford it right now."

"Baby, if you wanted to go for a short visit, I will try to somehow help you out."

"I don't know if it's wrong of me to think so but I almost feel like he deserves to be punished. For the way he treated us when we were young. For all the neglect and heartache. For our family falling apart."

"Baby, you don't mean that, do you?"

"I don't know. One part of me does and the other wants him to recover as soon as possible."

"Don't think like that. He is still your family. They are still your family. They need you."

He sighed loudly and hid his head in the arch between my shoulder and my face. I stroked the back of his head with my hand. It was late and we were both extremely tired. Still cuddling on the narrow bed, we quietly fell asleep.

The next morning I woke up as the sun shone through the window at the head of my bed. I looked over at him. He looked like an innocent child sleeping with his head on my left arm. I leaned over and kissed his forehead, then gently pulled my arm from underneath his head. Quietly and cautiously I got out of bed and headed for the shower. When I came out I noticed he was already awake.

"How are you feeling this morning, sleepy head?" I asked.

Still lying on the bed, he responded, "Yeah, okay."

"Do you want to stay for breakfast?"

"No, baby. I have to head back to the apartment, freshen up and head to uni."

"Will you be calling your family later today?"

"Yes. I have a three-hour break in between classes. I'll come back to the apartment and call to see how dad is doing. It will be morning in Dhaka by then."

"Alright, then. Make sure you call me if you need anything or you want to talk, OK?" I said, kissing him on the lips.

"OK." He responded kissing me back, and then jumped out of bed.

After I walked him to the front door and we said goodbye, I dressed for university. I had a quick breakfast and walked out to the tram stop. As I got on the tram, I sent him a message to make sure he was doing alright. I was worried about him. He wasn't very good at handling a crisis. He needed all the support I could give him. I needed to support him emotionally to help him stay strong. Otherwise he often went into a downward spiral where everything looked bleak.

In the evening, when I returned home from university, I decided to drop by his apartment. He was there, sitting at his computer. I enquired about his day and he told me he didn't go to class after all. He was at the apartment all day. He didn't even call home to check how everyone was. He didn't have lunch, only some fruits I had left out on the table the day before. Hearing all this, I went into the kitchen, got out some leftover pasta from the fridge and heat it in the microwave oven. I brought him a bowl of pasta and a glass of water. Putting them on the table in front of him, I urged him to eat up so we could call his family. After he was done, he dialled the number for his mother's mobile, speaking only briefly. He then passed the phone onto me. I spoke with her, enquired after her health and that of her husband's. I let her know we were praying for his quick recovery and passed on my best wishes for the family. I then gave the phone back to him so he could say goodbye.

After our phone conversation, my partner tried to start working on a university assignment. However, he found it difficult to concentrate. He looked dark and gloomy. I tried to cheer him up.

"You heard your mum. Your dad is going to be okay." I offered some comfort.

"I hate this stupid assignment. I am awful at my studies. I hate my job. I hate my life. Everything sucks."

"Come on, baby. Things aren't that bad. You are doing better at university than before. And I thought you liked working where you are now." I left out the part where I also thought that he had a partner who loved him and for many that was something to be appreciative of.

"I am a failure. You deserve much better."

"Where is all this coming from?" I asked in an empathetic tone of voice. I wanted to know.

"You know it's the truth," he emphasized.

"No, it's not. You are just saying all these because you are upset. Come on, we need to cheer you up!" I tried to sound cheerful, hoping it would somewhat help lighten his mood.

I walked over to his computer and opened the website for Hoyts cinemas. I opened the page consisting of the schedule for the movies being shown that evening.

"Here, have a look." I said turning my head towards him. "Which movie do you feel like watching?"

"I can't afford it right now," he responded.

"It's my treat. Come on! We need to get you out of this apartment and those pyjamas." I often received movie vouchers from work for my consistent performance, most of which were spent on him.

Luckily he didn't need much convincing. He looked at the monitor to pick a movie. We left the apartment twenty minutes afterwards to be able to catch the movie he had picked at the nick of time. It was a thriller. We both enjoyed the complex plot that kept us guessing every step of the way. It was the perfect movie to take his mind off the reality. By the time the movie had ended, we were both starving. It was already rather late. There was a diner-style burger joint at the cinemas that he loved. After the movie, I suggested we have dinner there. He had his usual steak burger and I had a vegetarian one. We shared a strawberry milkshake. I fancied their milkshake which came in a large '60s diner-styled tin tumbler. When we drove back to his apartment after dinner, I could see that his spirits had visibly lifted. Even if it was so, I knew he didn't want to be on his own that night as much as I didn't want to leave his side. I stayed the night.

Chapter 14

"*B*aby, I know this is a week night and you have uni tomorrow morning, but do you want to come over tonight?" a voice pleaded to me over the telephone.

My boyfriend and I were into the second year of our relationship. He had moved into an apartment which was less than ten minutes from where I lived because the time it took to travel had started to get to us. I was constantly juggling my time between university studies, part-time work, my family and him. He was doing the same between his studies, part-time work and our relationship. We hated not being able to see each other as much as we would like, which meant we would see each other exactly as much as we wanted. Even if that equalled driving for an hour to get to the other after a long day at university and work, while driving back almost half-asleep in the middle of the night to get ready to do it all over again the following day. Finally, we decided it would make more sense for us to live closer together. Since my family would not allow me to move in with him, and his family would not appreciate it either even if they were thousands of miles away, the easiest thing to do was for him to find a one-bedroom-apartment in our vicinity. It was also a lot closer to his university, so it worked out perfectly. We always made time for each other, no matter what the circumstances were.

"Babe, I have both university and work tomorrow. It is going to be a really long day so I was hoping I could stay at my place tonight." I responded, aiming to be more rational than romantic, even though I was dying to see him.

"So you don't want to see me tonight?" teased the voice on the other end. "You know you want to. Plus, I really miss you. I do."

"Okay, yes, I want to!" I gave in as I knew I would. "See you soon."

"Love you."

After hanging up, I packed some clothes and my make-up into a small shoulder bag and quietly left the house. I took my car even though I could have just as easily walked. I was planning on leaving for university directly from his apartment the next day rather than returning to mine. Normally I took the tram to university but drove if I had work afterwards, later on in the day. Public transport became less frequent in the evenings—catching a tram back home after work would take me up to an hour while driving would only be twenty minutes at the most. It was already rather late, so I was hoping to spend about a half-hour keeping him company and swapping our daily stories before being able to head to bed. I was exhausted.

As I entered his apartment with the set of keys he had given me when he first moved in, I saw him heating up his dinner. He usually ate late, and stayed up later than I did.

"You are here!" exclaimed my boyfriend, giving me a kiss. "Just heating up the chicken you made for me last night. It's delicious!"

"Thanks! How was your day?" I asked as I walked towards the bedroom to drop my bag in there.

"Hmmm . . . okay I guess. I didn't make it to the first class today. Couldn't get out of bed. Work was really busy though."

"Babe, you know you have to try harder this semester, right? You need to pick up your grades." It was the pep talk I had given him too many times before.

"I know, I know. Anyway, how was your day?" he reciprocated.

"Well, got that assignment back—the one I was working on all night last Thursday. Remember, the one I couldn't put too much time into because of the group project that needed to be completed?"

"Yeah, yeah. How did you go?" he asked enthusiastically.

"Ummm, I got a high distinction!" I replied with a big smile on my face.

117

My boyfriend came towards me and said, "I knew you could do it," as he squeezed me tight.

We talked more about random things as we often did, while he ate his dinner in front of the television with the volume turned down. After he finished, he headed towards his computer to work on an assignment due the next day. I started to get ready for bed when he asked me if I was able to make some suggestions on the assignment he was working on. I had done a similar subject the semester before, and even though we didn't go to the same university, the theories were the same. I sat with him for fifteen minutes to give him some pointers, then kissed him goodnight. As I was leaving the room to head towards the bedroom, I saw him staring at some late night show on the television. I did not know what the show was about, but seeing that the host of the show was a gorgeous brunette, I teasingly said, "Ooh, she is hot! Just your type of girl. Don't let her distract you from your assignment for too long. Love you! Good night!"

"What are you trying to say?" he wondered.

"Just teasing you, baby. 'Night!" I called out again.

"No, no, I know you. You weren't 'just' teasing. Come back here!"

"I am really, really tired babe. I need to get to bed." I responded, reluctant to continue on with the conversation any longer.

"What did you mean by 'your type of girl'?" he probed.

"Well ... tall, brunette, long hair, skinny, well-endowed ... your type of girl." I explained with a smile on my face, teasing him once more, as I walked towards him.

"You think I am always checking out other girls, don't you?"

"No, not always. It's normal if you do though. Don't deny it."

"I can't even watch a TV show in peace. Why are you always so jealous?"

"Oh my god! I am not jealous! I was just trying to tease you like I always do with everyone else. It's not a big deal. Just get back to your assignment."

"No, no, no. I know you," he was starting to sound a little angry now.

"Well clearly you don't," I responded. "I am going to bed."

"What is your problem? You don't trust me, is that it? You are always thinking I am checking out girls on TV, girls in shopping malls ..."

I cut his sentence short. "Look. I was just teasing you right then, but when girls do look at you in malls it's not like I don't see you returning their looks just

119

because you are towering over me. I am not jealous; I just call it as I see it."

"So you just want me to walk around blindly on the streets."

"Well, there is a difference between just looking at someone and really looking at someone. Especially when I am right there next to you, and you make it so obvious sometimes, it hurts."

"You never check out any guys while you are out and about with me, or without me?" he challenged.

Thinking about it for a moment, I responded surprising even myself at the truth, "Actually, now that I think about it, no. I can't even remember the last time I saw someone on the streets that caught my eye and made me go 'whoa!' It just hasn't happened."

He raised his voice. "You are a liar. I don't believe you. How can you even have the guts to come over to my house and insult me like this? Get out!"

"Are you serious?" I asked surprised at the extreme reaction he was having.

"I said it's my house and I don't want you here tonight. So, get out!" Now he was shouting so loud I was sure even the neighbours could hear him. The veins on his forehead began to pop.

"Your house? So that's how it's going to be from now on, is it?" Now I was starting to get upset. "I thought it was ours."

"Well, you thought wrong. Now get out."

"Aren't you over-reacting a little?"

"Don't tell me how I should or should not react. Stop telling me how to be. You have crossed the line."

"Baby, it's late and I'm exhausted. Sorry, I didn't mean it as it came out. Can we just forget about the whole thing, please?"

I hated leaving after an argument with a bad taste in my mouth. I knew what usually came afterwards—a game on the battle of power—a game about who should contact who first, who would be the first to give in. I despised those games. I would rather try to call truce right now, than stay mad at each other for a few days only to arrive at the same conclusion. I felt my energies were better utilised elsewhere like my studies or my work. So, I was happy to cut corners and give in right then. Even though I knew in my heart that I just wasn't imagining things, I also knew dishing such criticism out loud only made the person sound paranoid.

"I really don't appreciate what you said before," he said sounding a little calmer than before.

"OK, OK. I said I'm sorry." Walking up to him I gave him a kiss on the left cheek. "Do you forgive me? I'm sorry."

"It better not happen ever again," came the response in a commanding tone.

He kissed me goodnight once more. I returned it, relieved to see him not as angry as I had made him earlier. I shut the door behind me as I walked into the bedroom, leaving him in the other room to work on his assignment. Then, *finally*, I crashed my head on the pillow.

Chapter 15

My partner and I decided to invite over a few of his friends for the first time to his apartment. It had already been several months since he moved in to the new apartment but we didn't have a house-warming to mark the occasion. I had never met any of his friends so it would be a good opportunity for me to get to know them. I had met some of his colleagues at a work Christmas function that he had taken me to, but I had never met the high school or university friends he would talk to me about. It was a little strange given he had met my best friends almost as soon as we had started dating, and he hung out with my family like they were his own. I did, however, know that when he was not working or at university he chose to spend all his time with me or take some personal time of his own. He would talk to his friends over the phone or on internet chat, but when it came to making plans to see them, he was reluctant. Besides, he was very complacent and somewhat lazy. So I thought it would be a good idea to make sure he had other human contact, especially that of friends, and not lead a solitary life or one too dependent on a single person.

On the day his friends were to arrive, he asked if I would cook for them. He had been cooking longer than I was so his food would have tasted as good as or better than mine. I, however, often found it difficult to say 'no' to the request of loved ones, especially if it was a simple one such as cooking. He requested a few traditional Bangladeshi dishes and would help me out with the preparation. We went grocery shopping during the day to buy all the ingredients we needed for the dinner. I started cooking mid-afternoon to have everything ready before the guests arrived late afternoon. The aroma of hot beef curry, chicken korma and *polau* (flavoured mildly-sweet rice with sultanas) soon filled every corner of the tiny one-bedroom apartment. He prepared the Caesar salad, then laid out some chips and dips on the dining table.

I had just started to put the finishing touches, tasting to ensure the right amount of spices had been used, when the first guest arrived. After a quick introduction, I ran back into the kitchen to make sure none of the dishes still on the stove were over-cooked. The remainder of the guests arrived quite late, which I was thankful for, given the beef took longer to cook than I had expected. By the time all of his friends had gathered, it was already time for dinner. I didn't get much of an opportunity to sit down and chat with them. As soon as everyone was present, I started to serve the food so they could still enjoy it while hot. They were sure to have been starving by then. I assumed that I could just talk to them while dining. While my partner entertained them, I set the table and handed out the plates. After making sure everyone had enough *polau*, chicken and beef curries on their plates, I sat down with a small serving of my own. Ten minutes into dinner, I noticed most of the serving platters were almost empty, so I got up and brought out some more. Every time my mother invited guests over, I had noticed this was the same situation she was in—rather than having an opportunity to mingle, she was mostly busy making sure there was enough food for everyone, and all the guests were well looked after. The entertaining was usually left up to my sisters and I while my mother was being hospitable. 'Being hospitable' in my household meant feeding your guests well. So I did not expect to do any less. As much as I wanted to get to know his friends, serving traditional food rather than finger-food or pizzas made it a little difficult to enjoy a long conversation. This was also the first time I was entertaining in such a manner. It was, what I had called earlier that day, my hosting of the first 'adult' dinner.

After dinner, while I was about to sit down and join the party, one of the guests informed they would be leaving soon. I had prepared a traditional dessert earlier similar to rice pudding, which I knew was a crowd-pleaser. So I got up again and ran back into the kitchen to serve dessert. I didn't want them to leave without tasting some. Given we didn't normally entertain guests, and were unlikely to do so on an on-going basis at this stage of our lives, we only had a limited number of plates, glasses, and cutleries. As I re-entered the kitchen, I realised I would have to wash all those used during dinner by hand first before I could serve up dessert. Doing so as quickly as I could, I called out to request the guests to stay a little longer. They graciously obliged. Once I did serve up the dessert it was obvious that they were glad to have stayed longer to taste it. Some even commented on how much they appreciated being fed traditional food, which they were denied living away from their families and with no time to cook themselves while studying. Everyone thanked me for my hospitality before saying goodnight. I was really happy that the guests seemed genuinely pleased when they left.

As my partner closed the front door after the last departing guest, I turned to him smilingly and said, "Looks like that went well!"

"What the fuck is wrong with you?" he responded, surprisingly angry.

"Huh? What do you mean?" I asked quizzically.

"Why the fuck were you being so rude? You hardly talked to any of my friends all night. Are they not good enough for you?" he shouted.

My mouth dropped open in disbelief. "If you and I both talked, who would serve dinner? You saw how I was running around."

"It's not that difficult to socialize for a minute," he said in a patronising tone.

"I did!" I emphasized. "I did talk to them while eating, and whenever I could in-between all the running around I had to do. You didn't even offer any help!"

"You didn't ask for it."

"I didn't ask because someone needed to keep the guests company."

"No, you didn't ask because you wanted to be rude and not talk to them. I was so embarrassed. I am never inviting them over again!" he shouted even louder than before.

I was exhausted from cooking and entertaining all day. I could not take the criticism any longer.

"Stop shouting. How can you be so ungrateful?" It was not a rhetorical question. I genuinely wanted to know.

"I don't care if the neighbours hear. I have an idiot of a girlfriend."

Tears started streaming down my face, more because of anger at being so unappreciated than sadness.

"I cooked all day, I looked after your guests to make sure they were well fed, I cleaned up. I made sure you got what you wanted—to impress them. But you are never satisfied. If I sat down and talked to them, you would complain I am being inhospitable. Doing what I had to do, you are calling me rude?"

"That's because you can never do anything right! Never be a hundred percent. And I thought you were happy to cook. Why are you complaining now?"

"I am not complaining!" I couldn't help but scream, "I am simply talking! I did all that but you don't show even a little bit of appreciation!"

"Our mothers and aunts never complained about having to cook for their families or guests. Our fathers and uncles never had to help. Why can't you be more like them, how a traditional Bangladeshi girl should be?"

"Well, that's because I don't want to be like them. My father did not kill himself to put me through an expensive private school so I could be just like others. I have a lot of respect for our mothers and aunts for being able to do what they do, but I am not them. I am not going to slave after you. I need an equal partner. The way you sound, you don't need a wife or a partner. You need a maid!"

As soon as I said those words, I saw his right hand coming down on my left cheek like a tonne of bricks. Within the matter of a split second my cheek started to burn like it hadn't burnt in over a decade. My sisters and I were used to being disciplined by our parents when we were kids, but I had never had anyone strike me as an adult. Engulfed in utter shock and forced by the thrust, I fell on the couch. I put both my hands over my face and started to wail like a child. As much as I hurt physically, I was hurt even more emotionally. I could not believe what had just happened.

A few seconds later, I heard my boyfriend kneeling down on the ground next to me. He pulled me towards him with both arms and laid my head on his shoulder.

"I am so sorry, baby. I am so very sorry," he repeated over and over again. "I don't know what came over me."

In between my sobs, I murmured, "Just go away. Leave me alone."

"Please, baby. It would never happen again. I promise."

"You are saying that now, but I know it will happen again. I can't be with someone who hits me."

"I am not a hitter, baby. I would never do that to you ever again. I hate to see you cry. Please don't cry."

I couldn't stop myself. I was thinking of what had just happened. I knew I had to break it off with him. I was as upset at the prospect of having to lose him as I was at what he had done.

"Baby, please, listen to me," he pleaded again. "Please forgive me, please. I swear on my mother's life, it will never happen again."

"I can't trust you anymore. How can I trust you again after this?" I asked, still sobbing.

"Please, baby, you know you can trust me. Please, look at me." He pulled my face up to look at him. "Please look at me. I am telling you the truth. I love you. I can't bear the thought of losing you. Who would I have if I lost you? Please forgive me."

He had tears in his eyes. His face was red, nose flared, lips puffed. He looked like he was about to burst out crying. He squeezed me tight and started to sob as he repeated over and over again, "I am sorry. I am so sorry."

I put my arms around him. I hated to see him cry. I believed him. I believed that he loved me, that he would restrain himself from such a thing happening again. I knew he didn't want to lose me. He had taken the first step—admitting he understood what he did was wrong. I only wished and desired that he be able to keep his word.

I wiped the tears off his face with the back of my right hand. He kissed mine away from my cheeks. He then carried me off the couch, walked into the bedroom, put me down gently on the bed and pulled the blanket over my body, tucking me in as if I were a child. He kissed me on the forehead.

"Try to get some sleep baby. I'll put the rest of the things away in the kitchen, switch off the lights and join soon. I love you. Good night."

"'Night", I responded in a croaky voice, knowing it would be impossible for me to get a sound night's sleep. I hoped that the sheer exhaustion from the events of the day would force my eyelids shut. I prayed that I would not be haunted by any nightmares.

Chapter 16

"Morning, sleepy head!" I mumbled as I cuddled closer to him.

"Morning, my gorgeous," he responded with a kiss on my lips. "What time is it?"

I fumbled for my mobile and then answered, "About eleven already."

"Hmm . . . I want to sleep in for a little longer. It's an awfully cold day!" he said as he pulled the blanket over his head and dragged me underneath it with him. He wrapped his arms around my waist with his legs around mine, as if I were a pillow, and dropped back to sleep.

I tried to sleep in for longer but couldn't. I was an active person by nature and being in bed until eleven in the morning was already late enough. It was compensated for by the fact that we went to bed extremely late the night before, but even so I couldn't stay in any longer. After about twenty minutes of lying there in silence, and failing to shut my eyes again, I slowly unwrapped myself from his embrace before getting out of bed. I walked quietly into the shower. After a long hot shower,

I got dressed and headed towards the living room. I wanted to wait for him to have breakfast together. Well, more like brunch given it was almost hitting noon. I made myself a hot cup of coffee while I waited for him to wake up, and sipped it slowly in front of the television. There wasn't anything interesting on the television usually on Saturday mornings, so I surfed the channels before landing on some music video show. The volume was turned down even though I had pulled the bedroom door shut.

Half an hour later I heard shuffling behind the door. I knew he was finally up, and grabbing his things for the shower. After ten minutes, I opened the bedroom door and peeked inside. He was out of the shower, getting dressed. Landing a kiss on his bare broad shoulders, I asked what he wanted to do for brunch.

"Do you want to drive to Highpoint and get something to eat there?" he asked in return.

Highpoint was a large shopping centre about fifteen minutes drive away from his apartment. It was somewhere we often hung out if the day was too cold, or too hot, to be outdoors but we needed to head out of the house for a bit. That's where we often went for our dinner and movie dates as well. In fact, that's where we would normally end up too if we wanted to go shopping but didn't want to drive all the way to the city centre. It had everything we needed—shops, food courts, cafes, restaurants, cinemas, as well as supermarkets. It had become 'our' spot.

"Great idea!" I responded. "I am in the mood for strawberry pancakes."

As soon as I said those words, my mobile rang. It was my mother on the phone. After I answered it, and heard what she had to say, I relayed the message to my partner.

"Baby, mum is asking if we wanted to go over to the house for lunch. She has made parathas, and curries."

"Yum! Definitely." He replied excitedly. "I am in the mood for curries."

"Guess we will leave the strawberry pancakes for another day."

"Don't worry baby. I'll make you some tomorrow morning."

"Promise?"

"Promise."

I was satisfied with the response. We got in his car and drove over to my house, just a few minutes away. The aroma of hot curries greeted us as we entered. My sisters were already at the dining table awaiting my mother to serve up her wonders. I walked in and helped my mother carry a steaming bowl of beef curry into the dining room from the kitchen. She grabbed the plate full of freshly made parathas. My partner joined my sisters at the dining table.

"Who wants tea?" I asked as I put down the bowl I was carrying on the table.

Four sets of right hands went up into the air. Walking back into the kitchen, I made five cups of tea and walked back with those on a tray. Handing a cup to each at the table, I took my seat next to my partner.

"How is your father doing?" my mother asked him.

"Much better now, thank you. He has improved a lot in the last few weeks."

"I called last weekend, but couldn't get through. I kept getting a busy tone on your mother's mobile."

"Yes, it is really difficult to get a line most days. I can only get hold of her when it's early morning there."

"OK. I will try again tomorrow," my mother advised.

"How is school, Romana?" my partner asked turning his head towards my younger sister.

"Good!" she answered, cheerful as always. "Bhaiya, do you want to play tennis with me after lunch?" Romana called my partner *'Bhaiya'* which was a Bengali word typically used for older brothers.

"For sure!" he said with genuine enthusiasm in his voice.

After lunch, the three of us headed out to the tennis court nearby. Romana had two sets of rackets. Neither I nor my partner was as good as Romana in tennis but we often joined her on the court to give her some practice. I sat this one out, while I watched them take on each other. I loved seeing how Romana and he interacted with each other. He was like the older brother she never had, and he treated her like a little sister. They teased each other, chased each other around the court, he pulled her hair, she hit him on the arm, and then went back to playing again. After being beaten in two straight sets, he decided to call it quits. We walked back to the house, my partner and I said goodbye to my family, and the two of us drove back in his car to the apartment.

While in the car, we started discussing sports and fitness. I enjoyed eating healthy but wasn't a big fan of exercising, unless it involved a few stretches in my bedroom. On the other hand, he didn't care about what he ate, would always say he needed to go to the gymnasium and never did, but loved playing sports. In our own ways we both managed to maintain our desired weight range. We both loved food but neither of us could be called heavy. In fact, because of how tall he was, it was almost like nothing he ate stuck. He was skinny. So I felt it was my duty to keep feeding him. When we first met, he was working out to build his muscles. I had thought he had the body of a swimmer—narrow waist with broad shoulders and toned arms. He didn't do so anymore but always complained about needing to get back into it. He also thought I should join a gymnasium.

"You need to start working out, baby. Tone up. Look at those chubby cheeks." He pulled my right cheek to emphasize.

"Really? You should count your blessings your girlfriend didn't let herself go like most of her friends in serious relationships."

"Like Teressa you mean?" he added satirically, referring to the mutual friend who had introduced us.

"Do you know I am actually thinner now than when we had first met? I used to be a size 8 but now I am a size 6. Besides there is nothing here." I replied, placing my left hand on my abdomen.

"Nah, that can't be right. I swear you are heavier now than before. I should know. I am the one often picking you up off the ground!"

"I got curious the other day because of how you are always telling me I need to be skinnier. So I called one of those weight loss programs they keep advertising on the TV. They asked for my height and weight. Guess what their response was when I gave those to them?"

"That you need to lose five kilos?" he teased, mocking me.

"No! They calculated my BMI and said I was statistically underweight!"

"Yeah, that's because their definition of the average weight is probably some high figure. This is an obese population after all. I will buy you one of those exercise balls so you can work out at home if you don't want to go to the gym."

"I don't know why you are always pushing this. I told you I had weight issues back in the eighth grade in high school. All the girls were scarily thin, granted it was Dhaka, but they made me feel overweight. The following year, I stopped eating all kinds of meat, eggs, carbs, and lived off just fruits and vegetables. I was so underweight, it was dangerous. I can't believe you still keep pushing this on me when you know how sensitive I am on the subject."

"I want the girl I want to marry to be perfect. What's wrong with wanting that?"

"Whatever happened to how you used to say to me how perfect I was for you when we first got together? Whatever happened to 'I will always love you just as you are?' You said I was your 'ideal' girl. Now you just want to keep changing me."

"As I always say, 'My way or the highway', baby. You don't like it, too bad." He remarked with a devilish grin on his face.

Caught up in the conversation, I hadn't even realised that we had reached the apartment a while ago. We had gotten carried away with the banter, sitting in the car, parked in front of the building. I opened the car door and stepped outside. I didn't want to get upset, but it truly made me mad. I was finally at a point in my life where I was comfortable with my body, oblivious to how I really looked. It wasn't an easy achievement, but I was finally starting to be confident in my own skin. Right at that moment though I couldn't shake off the thought if most of my colleagues were generally greeting me with a 'hey sexy', why was my boyfriend always criticising my body. It wasn't just my weight. He would comment about some tiny scars I had from the time I had contracted chicken pox in my early teens. Why couldn't he just be satisfied? Leaving him sitting in the car, I shoved the passenger's side door shut and headed up the stairs to the apartment. Once I was in the bedroom, I couldn't help myself. I promised I wouldn't let any boy make me feel this way, but I found myself staring at my reflection in the mirror.

May be I could lose a bit off my thighs . . . and I did never like my arms. It wouldn't hurt to tone them up a bit, I thought. I looked intently at the reflection. Before I knew it, my old demons had started to creep back in.

Chapter 17

"*I* am so soooo excited about this trip! I need a break real bad!" I said to Romana as I packed my bags. One more night of sleep and then we would be on our way!

My partner and I were going away for the weekend, for a much needed holiday. We booked ourselves into a Bed & Breakfast at the Grampians National Park, which had been one of my most favourite destinations to get away in Melbourne for many years. It had mountains, forests and waterfalls. Whenever I felt like disappearing into nature, this was the hide-away I thought of immediately, away from the crowd and craziness of the city. The only thing missing was the sea, which I didn't quite mind, given I lived pretty close to the beach as it was and could drive by whenever I wanted to. Grampians was a few hours' drive away from the Central Business District, so whenever I wanted to go there, I would need to stay at least a night, but preferably longer. If I was crunched for time, two nights would be ideal to allow me to relish all that nature had to offer and take my mind off reality.

The accommodation was booked for Friday and Saturday nights. We were planning on returning by

Sunday afternoon to allow my partner to go to work later that the day. We were going to take my car for the road-trip so I was planning on driving over to his apartment tonight. That way the following morning we could wake up early and leave from his place straight away. It would give us more time to explore the Grampians, rather than spend it lazing around at home. I packed a couple of T-shirts, one blouse, a pair of jeans, a pair of shorts, my runners, some underwear and the necessary toiletries in a large shoulder bag. I decided to wear the pyjamas to his house instead of packing those. After all, I was going to be sleeping in them in less than a couple of hours. I could pack them tomorrow morning when I got changed into my jeans before leaving for the long drive. When my bag was packed, I gave Romana a kiss on the cheek, said goodbye to mum and headed out the door with the bag and my car keys in my hand. Sumara had still not returned from her dinner date that evening.

I drove to my partner's apartment, found on-street parking right outside and parked the car. I grabbed the bag from the car knowing I would need it to get ready the next morning. I walked up the stairs and used my set of keys to open the front door. I peeked inside. My partner was at his usual spot in front of the computer, sitting in his comfortable swivel chair, staring at the monitor. I tip-toed inside, quietly snuck up behind him, and kissed his neck.

"Hello!" he exclaimed, swivelling his chair to face me, and grabbed my waist with both hands. He pulled me towards him so hard it caused me to fall on his lap. I dropped the bag from my hand and wrapped my arms around his shoulder.

"How is my baby doing? Is he all set for the weekend getaway?" I asked, beaming from ear to ear.

"So ready!" he replied enthusiastically as he poked my nose with his. "Did you bring everything you would need—toothbrush, toothpaste, towels, clothes, undies?"

"Yep. I brought everything except for the towel. I'll take the spare one I keep here."

"Cool. Well I'm all packed too! I took the bottle of sunscreen as well that we bought the last time, just in case we need it."

"Perfect! Have you packed any food?"

"Umm, no actually."

"We will need to pack some snacks for the road. And water. Let me have a look in the kitchen to see what we can take with us."

I began to stand up, when he pulled me back down and landed a kiss on my very distinctive collar bone. He nibbled my ears for a few seconds, then kissed me on the lips before squeezing me tight. When he let go, I stood up, ruffled his hair with my right hand, and walked towards the kitchen. I opened all the cupboard doors one by one to check what snacks we had in stock that we could take with us. I found a bag of potato chips, a bag of snake lollies and a box of crackers. I shoved them into a recyclable shopping bag. I grabbed a couple of apples and oranges each from the kitchen counter and dropped them into the bag as well. I looked for the spare empty bottles we often kept stocked in the cupboard and filled one with water from the tap. I placed the bags and the bottle of water on the table in the dining room, ready to be picked up the next morning.

When I was done, my partner shut off his computer and headed with me to the bedroom. He set his alarm for seven in the morning before jumping into bed. We cuddled and fell asleep almost immediately. The radio went on at seven, waking us up from our sleep. There was some talk show on which I had never heard before. Still keeping his eyes shut, he switched off the radio alarm and made the usual noise he made that would tell me he was not ready to get out of bed yet. I knew I would have to get up first, as always, get ready, and wake him when we would absolutely need to leave the house. Kissing his forehead, I slowly snuck out of bed, grabbed my towel and walked into the shower. Once I had my shower, dried my hair, changed into my jeans and T-shirt, and put some light make-up on my face, I called my partner to wake him up. As he got up and went into the bathroom, I went in to the kitchen to prepare breakfast. I toasted a couple of slices of bread for myself and spread some strawberry jam on top. For him, I put four bars of Weet-Bix into a bowl and poured some milk on top. I also made two cups of hot tea with milk and sugar. I took them into the living room two at a time and put them on the coffee table. I switched on the television as I started on my breakfast. My partner joined within a minute. It only took us less than fifteen minutes to finish our breakfast. As I washed the dishes, my partner grabbed the car keys as well as both of our bags to drop them into the booth of the car. He then came back upstairs to check that all the windows and doors were shut, before we both headed downstairs to the car. Once we were seated in our respective seats, he leaned towards me and gave me a long kiss.

"Here is to relaxing and being one with nature!" he cheered as he inserted the keys into the ignition.

He started the engine and pulled onto the street. I fastened my seatbelt and dropped the back-rest of my seat as far back as it would go to make myself comfortable. I took my sunglasses out of the handbag, put them on and closed my eyes. His iPod was hooked into the stereo system of the car. As music filled the silence and crisp morning air blew through the open car windows, I dozed off to take a brief nap. When I re-opened my eyes, we had covered more than half the distance to the Grampians. I reached out to the back seat and pulled at the bag with the snacks and fruits in it. I opened the packet of lollies, and stuffed a snake into his mouth. Then I grabbed a couple and shoved them into mine. I was addicted to lollies, especially while on long drives.

Another hour later we reached our destination. After we checked into the Bed & Breakfast, and dropped off our bags, we drove to Halls Gap, a near-by town, for lunch. I was craving fish and chips. We only paid ten dollars for enough chips to feed four, two fillets of grilled fish and two cans of coke. We found ourselves a park bench to enjoy the lunch. As I sat down on the bench and spread my legs in front of me, I looked up to take in the surroundings. It was serene and beautiful. The sky was a crystal blue with some white clouds floating about which reminded me of fluffy cotton wools. Tall trees of all kinds enclosed the park through which I could get a glimpse of the green mountains beyond. The air I breathed in was so fresh it insinuated of true remedy for stress. There were pigeons everywhere, including the park bench we were sitting on. Apart from their chirping, there was no other noise or any form of sound I could hear. I smiled at myself, thinking this was exactly the reason why I loved to get away into the wilderness once in a while. It was calming.

I squeezed some of the lemon that was given to us with the fish and chips onto both the fillets, then spread a little bit of tartar sauce onto mine as well. My boyfriend opened a few sachets of the salt and pepper to pour them across the chips. As soon as everything was ready, we dug in. The chips were hot and crispy. I cut the fillet into small pieces and continued to put them into my mouth one after another as we sat silently enjoying the tranquillity. In between every slice, I would stuff a handful of chips into my mouth. I enjoyed the taste of freshly-cooked warm crispy chips. However, regardless of how hard we both tried to finish off all the food we had bought, it was impossible to do so. We managed to get through the fillets and only half the chips. After that we had to abandon the rest. It was just too much for the two of us. We fed a little of it to the pigeons and then threw out the rest in the trash bin, when we got up to return to the car. Once in the car, he opened up the map we had of the locality to check how we could make our way to the waterfalls.

We drove through the rugged countryside and steep mountains, with tall trees overarching each road, to arrive at the car park where all travellers would have to leave their car and make it the rest of the way to the waterfalls on foot. We disembarked, grabbed the bottle of water we were carrying in the car and set off to find the biggest of the three waterfalls in the region. After over half an hour of walking through the forest, and climbing down a large set of iron stairs over the side of the mountain, we got a glimpse of the waterfall we were searching for. Yet another fifteen minutes later we arrived at the foot of the waterfall, all sweaty and gasping for breath. However, it took us only a few sips of the bottle of water we were carrying with us and listening to the soothing sound of the flowing water as it thrust over the ground below, to feel rejuvenated. I handed over my watch and the camera to my partner and made my way closer to the bottom of the waterfall. Finding a spot safe enough to stand on, I posed for the camera. After a few shots while still dry, I made my way even closer to the water to get myself soaked in it. I was incredibly careful to make sure I didn't slip and fall. The rocks were slippery and could be treacherous. Once I found my footing, I closed my eyes and faced upwards to feel the cool thrust of the water against my entire structure. It was eerie and enchanting at the same time. I felt the chill down my spine and all over my body. The water was cold and pure, untouched. I felt as though I could stand like that forever, let the water wash away all my worries and dilemmas. It was only when I struggled to breath because of the severe force with which it was falling, that I had to move away from it.

I walked over the rocks carefully to find my bearing and made my way to the flat surface where my partner was waiting for me. Once I approached him, he handed me the camera to show the photos he had taken. I didn't realise that he kept clicking away while I was lost in the moment underneath the waterfall. There were some really incredible shots—a solitary soul lost in nature, obliviousness to the world around. I was impressed. I kissed him on the right cheek and asked him to pose for a few of his own. My photos might not turn out as artistic as his but he had no photos of himself during the trip, so I wanted to capture some. I also asked a man nearby if he could take some photos of the both of us together. It ended up giving us one of our favourite photos of the trip—a happy couple holding hands and smiling, with the marvellous waterfall a vision in the background. We sat down on the ground afterwards and rested for a while before making our way again towards the car park. The sun started to set as we drove from the park towards our accommodation deep in the forest.

The ride back to the Bed & Breakfast was a little dangerous. It was a steep drive down the mountain, in the dark. My partner was driving slower than he normally would but not slow enough. I urged him to go slower, but it fell on deaf ears. The sun had already set by now and the roads weren't well-lit. It was pitch dark all around. With all the rocks and other obstacles on the way, the ride was rather bumpy. After one such jerking of the car, when the front wheels hit against a large rock, I nearly jumped out of my seat and glared at my partner. While I turned my head sideways to look at him, I noticed something out of the corner of my eye. It looked like a body standing upright, hidden amongst the trees. I couldn't tell if it was that of a human or an animal, and if it was that of an animal, it was definitely unpredictable which animal. I just noticed something tall in the shadows hurling towards our car. I screamed and asked my partner to stop the car. In complete utter shock, he pushed heavily on the brake pedal. The engine roared, the car jolted, and then came to a sudden stop.

"Are you fucking out of your mind?" My partner screamed at me.

"There was something over there. I saw something over there." I responded in a timid voice, slightly shaken.

"What? I don't see anything, you idiot." He reproached.

Just as he uttered those words, the moving body came into full view as it stepped in front of the car headlights, but only for a moment. We were finally able to make out what caused such a stir—a kangaroo! The kangaroo had been waiting in the bushes on the side of the road, waiting for some light so it could see well enough to cross the road. Realising what had just happened, I was about to burst out laughing. However, the look on my partner's face stopped me. His nose had flared up, his eyes wide open, his teeth clenched. He was fuming.

"I asked you to slow down, didn't I? There are lots of wild animals and barely any light. You should have been more careful." I tried to reason with him.

"That's enough! You frightened the shit out of me!"

"Sorry I frightened you. I didn't mean to. It was an instant reaction."

"You know how dangerous it could have been if I lost control of the car?"

"Yes, I do! But what if you hit the poor kangaroo? What then?"

"Argh! Just shut the fuck up!"

Now I was genuinely upset. His frivolous use of the f-word and talking to me like I was an imbecile made me angry.

"Stop cursing at me! I hate, hate, hate, the way you always talk to me when things are a little out of whack!"

"Why are you with me then if you hate it so much?"

"Good question! I should be asking myself the same thing!"

He re-started the engine. Even the roar of the engine sounded like all hell was about to break loose. A painful silence accompanied us the rest of the way to our accommodation. As soon as we got into our room, he washed up and went straight to bed without saying a word. He turned sideways to face away from me and crossed his arms across his chest. Once I was ready for bed, I quietly duck underneath the covers. Even though the night was anything but chilly, the bed felt cold. We were both turned away from each other, with enough space in-between to sleep a third person. I felt a shiver down my spine. My heart was heavy. I felt lonely even though there was a person lying right next to me. It was harder to have someone next to me who I wanted to cuddle but couldn't, then to have no one at all. I lay on the bed silently for what felt like hours, before I finally fell asleep.

When I woke up, my partner was already awake. As I opened my eye-lids I hoped he had calmed down by now and we could enjoy the rest of what was left of our weekend get-away. I sat up straight on the bed. What I saw took me by surprise. His bag was near the front door, all packed.

"Good, you are up. Get ready. We are going back home. I have had enough of this weekend." He said in a harsh tone of voice when he noticed I had woken up.

"What?" I stammered in disbelief.

"I said let's go. Right now. I don't want to discuss this any further."

I considered for a minute if I should try to make him see some sense. I concluded though that if he didn't want to stay with me, I wasn't going to force him. I didn't want to be here either if he was going to be such bad company. This wasn't what I had in mind when I thought of getting away with the man I loved but this was how it turned out. I wasn't going to fight the truth anymore. I got out of bed, packed as quickly as I could, changed into appropriate clothing, brushed my teeth and jumped in the car, without saying a single word the entire time. He joined me a few minutes later. We drove up to the reception for the Bed & Breakfast, where he stopped for a few minutes to hand in the keys to our room, then we headed off towards the direction of Melbourne. We only made one stop on the way for lunch, neither of us talking to each other throughout the journey. Once we reached his apartment, he got out of my car without saying goodbye, leaving my car keys in the ignition. I climbed into the driver's seat and started the engine. I was too upset to go home, so instead I started to drive towards Williamstown beach. I drove slowly as it felt like I was being smothered by a billion scattered thoughts. When I reached my destination, I parked the car overlooking the water and sat there in silence. I was so deep in my thoughts, I didn't even notice when the sun had set.

I started up the engine when I realised it was getting too dark to stay parked where I was. I decided it was time to go home. However, as I drove towards my house, I had a sudden feeling of shame engulf me. I didn't want to have to answer to my family why I had returned a day early, and I didn't want to have to lie. In fact, I just didn't feel like seeing anyone right then or being confronted. I wanted to be completely alone. Realising this, I changed my direction and headed towards the city centre instead. I was going to find a hotel to stay the night. It would help me clear my head. When I got to the centre, I checked at least a dozen hotels. There was not a single room available. It was a Saturday night and a busy time of the year. Tourists were flocking to Melbourne from all over the world. I expected to find at least one room, even if it might have been highly priced. But no. Given my luck, there was nothing. Absolutely nothing available at all.

Feeling exhausted and betrayed by fate, I drove around to look for a narrow, dark alleyway where I could park my car and no one would notice me. I found one very soon, where there were no people around. A large rubbish bin stood solitarily at the end of the alley. I parked on one side, to make sure if any car did happen to drive into the alley way, the driver had the ability to make a turn and head back out. I switched off the headlights, and checked to make sure all the doors were locked. Then, after a few moments of rehashing the events in my head, I just started to cry. After a while, my cry turned to a sob as I began to calm down a little. The overwhelming emotions however soon made me so exhausted that I dozed off to sleep. The noise of a truck backing into the alley way woke me up. I opened my eyes and rubbed them with both hands. I saw a rubbish truck entering the alley way and heading towards the large bin only a few meters away from my car. The first few rays of the sun shone through my window. I had slept for hours. The city would be awake in a few moments, making it difficult for me to keep hiding away for much longer. I needed to face reality. I decided it was time to go home.

Chapter 18

I had no idea of the day that was ahead. On the outset, it was like any other day during summer vacation—no classes, therefore working insane hours. I had a full day at work, a total of eight and half hours. Given I normally worked part-time while classes were on, it was a struggle for me to adjust to working a full day during the holidays. I knew that's what I had to do today, but I was in no way prepared for it. When I woke up in the morning, I felt really unsettled. I didn't feel like going to work. I just wanted to stay in, in my pyjamas, eat junk food in front of the television and be a couch potato. My shift started at mid-day. At about eleven in the morning, I thought about calling in sick but soon after changed my mind. I needed to get out of the house.

I finally managed to drag myself out of the couch about half past eleven. Already running late for work and with no time to spare, I quickly changed into what I could get my hands on, grabbed the car keys and rushed out the door. I pulled out of the driveway in a hurry. I was already thinking I shouldn't have left home so late. It was really important to maintain a perfect adherence that week. There was a lot happening at work, so getting in late was not going to be looked upon favourably. I was driving faster than I normally would. I had the music on loud. I was distracted, thinking of the events of the day before. It was the reason why I was so upset and so unmotivated. A fight with my partner the day before had me on edge.

I could not recall all the details of how the fight got started. I just remembered how upset we both were at each other when he asked me to leave his apartment and I stormed out. I don't know what small incident started it all but it ended with some concerning issues being raised about our families. He was disappointed in me that I did not take the initiative to call his mother and talk to her every Sunday like, according to him, a good Bangladeshi girl should. I was angry at him for taking stabs at my beloved sister, Romana, for being how social she was. He thought she had too many friends, hung out too much, and needed to be set a curfew, in order to be disciplined. This made me really upset because my sister might have been social but was smart enough not to ever do anything that would hurt her or others. I knew for a fact that she was an all-rounder, who maintained her grades even if she hung out with her friends often, worked really hard at her job even though she was still in high school. She had a great relationship with all her friends as well as her family. So I did not understand how being social could be looked upon as a negative trait. I also didn't think it was appropriate for him to be criticising my sister, inadvertently criticising how my mother had raised her, or how Sumara and I, as her older sisters, might have influenced her.

Neither did I agree that it was an obligation for me to speak to his mother every Sunday. I believed I should speak when I could but because I cared, not because I was obliged to. I was not a big fan of long distance conversations. In fact, I was not a big "chatter" on the phone, even with my friends. This was another way my father had tried to discipline his children, not allowing us to use the phone unless it was an emergency. While my friends would jump on the phone as soon as they got home straight after school for idle gossip, I would be asked to stay away and par take in something more productive. At this point, I did make an effort whenever I could to speak to his family. It was not just for his sake, but also because I wanted to. However, the conservations could hardly be lengthy given I never had the chance to really get to know them personally, and as far as they were concerned, I was only their son's girlfriend.

After I left his apartment in distress, he went to work as he did every Sunday afternoon. I was secretly hoping he would give me a call when he returned home that evening so we could calmly talk things over. I hated having unresolved issues hanging over my head. I couldn't speak for him, but I genuinely disliked fighting. It was depressing. I preferred to make up as soon as we possibly could, but he was better at holding a grudge. So this time I decided that I needed to stand my ground. He had said a lot of things that were uncalled for. I could bare it if it was about me, but because it involved the family member I loved the most, I couldn't. He didn't call me that night, nor this morning and neither did I call him. My heart was in a knot. As I now drove to work thinking about the events of the day before over and over in my head, I started to think that maybe he was right. May be I did need to change. I needed to accept certain things as my responsibility now that I was in a serious relationship. May be he had a point about my sister too and I didn't want to see it because in my eyes she could do no wrong. I was still quite anxious behind the wheel of my car when I had the sudden feeling that I should slow down. I had been driving a tad over the speed limit since I left home. I was in a hurry to get to work. I had just turned left to get onto the main road that would take me straight to the office, when I had a sudden flash. A flash that I was in an accident. Even though I was too preoccupied with other thoughts to pay enough attention to that feeling, I slowed down to under the speed limit. The Alicia Keys album I had inserted in the CD player was still blasting loudly from the speakers of my car.

As I approached the next set of traffic lights, the lights changed from green to amber. I put my foot on the brake pedal to bring the car to a halt at the intersection. As my car started to slow down, something I saw at the corner of my eye took me by immense surprise. It was a van, a white van. It was approaching towards me from the next lane, on the right of the driver's side. As the lights changed again from amber to red, the van veered towards my lane, barely leaving any distance between the tip of my bonnet and the edge of its boot as it approached. If it came any closer, I would be squashed into oblivion, my body parts scattered onto the road in a thousand pieces. I saw the van getting closer every millisecond through the window on the driver's side. My life flashed before my eyes as I decided to steer my car away from a disastrous end to the affair. I swerved, trying to escape my imminent fate, but struck the traffic pole on the side of the road. The thrust of it caused my car to spin sixty degrees clockwise, before coming to a sudden halt. I was shaken up but otherwise unharmed. My car was not so lucky. The heavy metal of the pole completely smashed the passenger's side of my car. I could only imagine what might have happened if there was someone in the other seat. The door protruded inwards, the side mirror crumbled into a million pieces, with half the bonnet on the left-hand-side totally disfigured. It looked like one of those cars at the wreckers' ready to be turned to scrap metal. The impact of it all affected the mechanism for the rest of the car. I tried to untie my seat belt but it was stuck. I pulled and pulled at it, before it finally gave in. I opened the door, and stumbled out of the car, still in utter shock. My favourite Alicia Keys' song "Fallin'" continued to blast from the speakers. I looked around. No one had stopped to offer a hand or watch what was going on. The van had fled the scene. I was on my own.

I wanted to dial my partner immediately for some comfort but I knew better. I knew all too well how he might respond. Instead, I dialled roadside assistance, to be a step ahead, and asked a tow truck to be sent out. Next I called work mentioning I had been in an accident so I could have the day off to manage the situation. As I waited for the tow truck to arrive, I called my partner. I explained briefly what had happened.

"Did you call for the tow truck?" he asked grimly.

"Yes." I responded.

"Have you called the police?"

"No."

"Call the police. Let them get a report. Then ask them to drive you home." He added in a patronising tone, "Drive more carefully next time. At least if the van hit you, you could have made a claim. Now it's all your doing."

My heart sank. What was I expecting? It's not like in the movies when accidents suddenly bring the loved ones closer together; they realise life is too short to be fiddling around with; they forget their differences and declare their love for each other. May be I was naïve like that, but not him. There had been circumstances before where I had actually prayed that something like this would happen, but with more drastic consequences, after an episode when my heart would be breaking and he showed no sign of remorse. I hoped that when we were having one of our arguments and he turned away putting all the blame on me, an accident or an illness would help him see light and bring me out of my misery. I was exhausted from all the mind games he would play with me following a fight, and I thought something like this would solve all our problems. Now that it had actually happened, it made me realise what things were truly like in the real world. In the real world, your partner who was angry with you still remained angry and said hurtful or careless things. I knew if we hadn't had the fight the day before, he would probably be supportive right now. But if he was angry at me, his reaction was always completely the opposite. I should have known better than to call him at all. I should have taken control of the situation solely on my own. Talking to him only made me more depressed. It was a wakeup call. A lesson learnt—to be more self-sufficient, to be more independent.

"At the end of the day, no one in the whole world would care about you as much as you. What was happening in your life was only important enough for you. Be strong even when you were in a relationship. Don't just take it for granted that your partner would be there for you in a crisis." I told myself.

I hung up and called the police. When the police arrived, I gave them a briefing of what had happened. They asked me a range of questions of which the most important I could not answer, the registration number of the van. One of the officers took some photographs of the scene. When the tow truck arrived, I gave the driver my address. He used the wheel-lift of the truck to drag my car onto the flatbed before securing it. After he left the site with my car, the police escorted me back home in theirs. I was advised they would be in touch with any progress if the driver of the white van could be tracked down. I thanked them and got out of the car. The tow truck had already arrived at my house by then. I showed the driver the parking space where he could leave my car. He left after I settled the large bill he presented me with.

When I turned the key in the keyhole and pushed my front door open, I had never felt lonelier than I did right then. It was strange because I still had my mother, my sisters, my friends and a boyfriend. Yet the event of that day made me feel like there was no one I could rely on in this world when I was in need. I did manage to send some text messages to my family in between handling the police and getting the car towed. They didn't seem too phased or offer any helpful suggestions with regards to my next course of action. As far as moral support was concerned, they would automatically assume that role was being filled by my partner. I started to feel that may be this relationship was distancing me from my family. I would need to make a more conscious effort to spend more time with them so they knew I wanted them to be as much a part of my life as he was. Different points of view about a lot of things between Sumara and my boyfriend were already driving her away. I did not want to alienate my mother and Romana as well.

Two hours after I got home, Romana arrived home from school. She asked me for details of exactly what had happened. I gave her a complete account of the accident. She responded with a tight hug, adding that she was glad I was physically alright. Then she enquired about how I was feeling. I could not hold back any longer. Tears burst out of me and I told her the truth about my mental state. I told her about how shaken up I was when the accident happened, how hurt I was at the reaction of my partner when I called him and how lonely I felt when I entered through the door after the accident. She handed me a tissue to wipe off my tears and squeezed me tight again. She made me a hot cup of tea while we talked some more.

Soon after I had finished drinking the tea, my mother arrived home from work. We decided we needed a family dinner that night, just the four of us. I suggested we get some take-away pizzas from the local pizza shop and pick up a box of ice-cream from the local supermarket. Romana called in early and ordered the pizzas—two barbecued chicken and one vegetarian, all large. I then took her to pick up the ice-cream before picking up the pizzas she had ordered. We stopped over on the way at the video store to hire a chick flick as well. Sumara arrived home just as I was pulling into the driveway in my mother's car. She didn't ask me about the accident. As soon as we entered the house with the large hot pizzas, the ice-cream and the movie, we sat down in front of the television with the food spread out on the floor. This was something we had not done in a very long time.

"Do you remember how we used to order pizzas and hire DVDs all the time when we first moved to Melbourne?" I asked my sisters.

"Yes. That was before you got your serious boyfriend, Romana her hundreds of friends and mum her busy work schedule." Sumara responded sarcastically.

"And before you got your 'I am too cool to spend too much time with my family' attitude." Romana added in a sly manner, casting a glance towards Sumara.

"It's more like my family is too cool for me!" Sumara replied back jokingly at her little sister.

"OK, come on now you girls!" my mother finally chipped in, handing out the serviettes for our pizza slices, as the movie title *"The Notebook"* appeared on the screen. "Let's dig in!"

Chapter 19

I was at the apartment on a weeknight waiting for my partner to return home from work. I had completed all my assignments for university early so I had time to cook him dinner. Normally I didn't enjoy eating curries all the time. I preferred to have variety—sometimes pasta, sometimes stir-fry vegetables or at other times just a simple salad. He, on the other hand, preferred more traditional food for dinner if we weren't eating out. So tonight I made him some rice, chicken curry, lentils, and spinach fried with garlic. I timed myself perfectly so that all the cooking would be done, and I would have time to clean the kitchen before he returned home from work. Half an hour before he was about to arrive, I found myself scrubbing the kitchen bench-top and the sink hard to make sure there were no stains. I wanted to leave everything shiny and tidy. I didn't want to give him even the slightest of reasons to be upset at how I had left things at the apartment. Everything needed to be perfect.

When he finally arrived home, I asked him how his day was. He told me stories about this situation at work that he had been dealing with for several weeks. Then he reciprocated with the same question. Ordinarily I would have given him a summary of everything I did that day as well as the detailed version of anything interesting. However, today, I simply responded that I came over to the apartment after university so I could cook him dinner. I didn't tell him much else. I walked over to the kitchen and served him food. He took the plate into the living room to eat to in front of the television. I joined him for an hour to watch the show that was on at the time, then said goodnight.

The same was repeated the next night, and the next. If there was left-over food already in the fridge from a previous night, it meant I only had to heat things up to get his dinner ready. This also meant fewer things to clean up. Therefore it gave me more time to do things that I needed to get done for myself. I didn't let my studies suffer no matter how hectic my personal life was. This was a crucial year for me. This was the year I would be applying for graduate positions to make sure I had a decent job offer for when my university degree was completed. I had my eye on the top consulting firms or one of the top financial institutions in the country. I needed to put the right amount of effort into completing my resume, focus on submitting the job applications on time, and complete any online psychometric tests that some companies might require. The psychometric tests weren't my strong suit. So I bought a couple of books to help strengthen my skills. I would practice the exercises from it when I finally managed to have a spare moment to myself or before heading to bed. Even though almost all the students in my course were busy applying for jobs, it didn't stop the university from handing out assignments more difficult than ever. I was spending my Saturdays completing group projects on university campus.

My partner would now and again complain how little time we spent on the weekends. So like everything else in my life at that point, I had to have a routine for my weekends as well. I was going to the campus on Saturday mornings when he would still be sleeping in. It helped that he would never get up before one in the afternoon. Saturday nights we would either go out or do something at home. Sunday mornings I spent at his apartment until he headed to work. I couldn't really call it 'quality' time apart from may be a nice breakfast or brunch together, because I spent most of that time doing household chores. He helped me out by vacuuming the apartment or taking out the garbage. I would do the cleaning, cooking, scrubbing and almost everything else. Sunday afternoons I would head over to my house when he left for work, and sit myself down in front of the computer to work on my job search. You only got less than a couple of months window to apply at all the organisations that you chose to, so depending on the number of firms you were applying at you either had a lot of time to apply or hardly any. No one would choose to apply at just one firm. That would be ludicrous. You needed to keep your options open.

Initially I thought of applying at the top four companies of each of the industries that I was even remotely interested in. It wasn't as simple as just sending through my resume and wishing for luck. Research was a key component of any application to ensure the cover letters demonstrated I knew the company well enough to know why I wanted to be a part of their team. Therefore I finally found myself crunched for time. I only managed to apply to less than half of the companies I had originally thought of applying to. It reduced my chances drastically of ensuring I landed an offer I couldn't refuse, so I did have to keep my fingers crossed. I wasn't looking forward either to the next steps if I managed to get through to the next round—the assessment centres for more psychometric tests and the multi-rung interview processes. I needed to be at the top of my game. Needless to say, these were stressful times.

As I started to realise my change in attitude towards the relationship, I assumed it was because I wanted to avoid confrontation of any kind with my partner. The less time I spent dealing with one mishap or another, the more time I had to focus on my future. If he found a reason to be upset at me, it required a lot of effort to sort things out. The result would either be that after spending a lot of time convincing him it would not happen again, he would understand, or that he wouldn't and I would be wasting time being devastated. I wasn't being cold about how I was dealing with the relationship. I was simply trying to preserve myself. Funnily enough he didn't even notice the change in my attitude towards it.

As I progressed through to the interviews, I received a lot of support from my family and my partner during the preparation period. They would always give me words of encouragement. On the morning of the interviews, the whispers of inspiration from my partner would be enough for me to be able to walk in with an aura of confidence and nail each interview. By then, I had forgotten I had any friends. I would pick up the phone and talk to them from time to time. However, any spare time I had was spent with my partner or my family. Most of them were in the same situation as I with the job search, so it was almost normal that we didn't get to hang out as much. Now and then I would bump into one at an interview, causing us both to be surprised that we had no idea the other would be attending the same, or that had even applied for the same position with the company. All of us just waited, rather impatiently, for this period of our lives to be over so things could soon return to normal. More importantly, we just wanted to know that we managed to secure a job for the following year. None of us wanted to sit idly for a year after graduation, jobless, waiting to re-apply to the exact same companies only a year later, especially when the job market was getting tougher.

Finally, in June that year, after almost three months of many rounds of job interviews, the letters started to arrive in the mail. One afternoon, I came home from university and was ecstatic to find a letter in my name from the consulting firm I had been dreaming of joining all throughout my bachelor degree. I was accepted. I needed to reply with my decision within two weeks. In those two weeks, I received two more offers from two of the top firms in each of their industries. I felt blessed with the choices but still had to make a tough decision. I needed to work out which company was a better fit for me for the longer term. I knew that, after all, when you started to work full time in these industries, you spent literally half or more of your day with your colleagues, a small amount of the remainder of the day with your loved ones and the rest sleeping. I needed to be sure of my choice.

Even though an important decision lay ahead of me, the more stressful times had passed. I was grateful to my partner for being so incredibly supportive. Whenever I thanked him, he would say it was his job and he was ecstatic with the result I had achieved. One evening though, during a conversation about our future, his tone changed. His real feelings came out. I couldn't believe what I was hearing. He sounded jealous and obnoxious on how things had turned out for me. He felt depressed at how things were progressing with him. I tried to comfort him. I was running out of advice to give him. I had tried everything to help turn things around for him—be it mental support or physically assisting him with getting the work done. It had reached a point where if he didn't help himself, no one else could. So I desperately tried to get him to understand and hoped he listened.

As the days went by, I still continued to do the household chores in the same manner as I had done when I was trying to avoid confrontation earlier of any kind. I would complete all the chores before he arrived home from work to make sure everything was in tip top shape. Dinner would be ready to be served, and kitchen left perfectly tidy. To that list soon was added grocery shopping for anything that was needed at the apartment but he couldn't make time to pick up during the week. I thought I was being helpful. I thought I was making sure he had time to focus on what was important and didn't feel depressed about what was lacking. One evening, as I was running late to complete my usual chores, I started to feel incredibly anxious. My heart started to beat faster and I was out of breath. I tried to pull myself together, not knowing the reason for my reaction. Something was bothering me, but I couldn't quite put my finger on it.

That evening he enquired about the chores I had left unfinished. He criticised me in a harsh voice as he would often do by then for my lack of competence. At first I didn't respond, but as he began to provoke me more and more I reminded him again how ungrateful he had become. I reminded him that everything I was doing for him was out of love and not as an obligation, but that he took these for granted. He simply assumed that it was my job to constantly provide for him and care for him. If anything wasn't to his liking, he would scrutinise me for it. I brought up my once verbalised theory about how he wanted a maid and not a partner. This enraged him like I had never seen him be enraged before. He lashed out more verbal abuse, grabbed me by the neck and threw me onto the bed. I roared up, saying once more he didn't have the right to treat me like this. He slapped me on my left cheek, then pushed me, and my head hit against the wall at the head of the bed. I started to moan and cry as the pain soared. He walked off into the living room, leaving me crouched over on top of the bed.

I lay there, crying like a wounded animal. When the cries turned to sobs, I wiped my face with a tissue. I took my car keys off the bedside table, grabbed my handbag and pushed open the bedroom door. Marching towards the front door, I barged out. As I stepped outside, almost about to slam the door shut behind me, I heard his voice roar.

"Where do you think you are going? You will never set foot in this apartment again if you leave tonight!"

Leaving his voice echoing behind me, I shut the door, ran down the stairs, into the car park and in my car. I drove for a couple of minutes until I was away from both his place and mine. I found a really quiet street in the neighbourhood with hardly any lights on to park my car. I sat there silently for a couple of minutes before the tears started to roll again. I couldn't help myself. I cried and cried. I thought about what my life had become, how my relationship was changing and how my man was becoming a more different person everyday who I recognised less and less. I didn't know what to do. I didn't know what I could do to change him back to how he used to be, in order to change our relationship back to how it was. I wanted help and guidance but didn't know where to turn to. I considered going to a therapist but soon gave up the idea knowing how expensive it might be. I still loved him but didn't understand why he acted so differently even though he claimed he still loved me too. I couldn't believe he raised his hand, even though he had promised it would never happen again. I felt desperate.

I didn't want to head home straight away feeling the way I was feeling. I waited a few hours in the car, sometimes sitting completely still, and at other times crying. At one point I felt so exhausted that I even dozed off for a little. Once I woke up, I checked my face in the mirror to make sure I looked presentable if my sisters happened to be awake at the house. I wiped my face several times and blew my nose into a tissue. Then I drove home. I quietly slipped into the house and headed straight to my room. Eventually that night while I lay in bed for hours unable to fall asleep, I figured out something about my state of being. I began to realise why I was nervous earlier that day. Even though I had protested and roared at his abuse during the confrontation, I wasn't feeling as strong as I had posed. I felt provoked so my reaction was to rebel but mentally I was in a completely different zone. In the past few years I had undergone a strange kind of metamorphosis—transforming from the type of person who had so much positive energy that they could light up a room just by entering it to someone introverted and confined within themselves.

The honest truth behind my state of mind was that I had grown to become scared dead of my controlling partner.

Chapter 20

The guests were beginning to arrive but none of the preparation was complete. I was almost as stressed out as a bride on her wedding day. My sisters were in charge of organising the program for the evening but they were still at the printers trying to get the programs printed. The printer at home broke down at the last minute. My mother was managing the caterers, and preparing the traditional desserts herself. The caterers were almost ready but the desserts were still in the oven. My best friends took charge of the decoration, which they started off rather late in the day after several hiccups. They were now rushing to put the final touches. My partner was in charge of overseeing sound, which he just managed to finish in time for the guests. However, he was still running late as he now needed to rush home to change into his suit. I was due to arrive at the hall in time to greet the guests with my partner at the door, and yet I was being worked on by the make-up artist who showed up at the house an hour late. I hit the panic button when Romana called to say the colleagues I invited from work that evening had already arrived. They didn't know anyone else at the event except each other, so I really needed to rush to the venue to make them feel welcome.

I asked the make-up artist to hurry up with doing my make-up or let me go as I was. I wouldn't look as perfect as I had hoped but I couldn't spend another hour or half sitting still while the guests were trying to keep themselves entertained. She rushed to do my hair as quickly as possible after hastily finishing my make-up. In the meantime, I called my partner to check on how he was progressing. He advised that he had already changed into his suit at the apartment and would be at the venue within twenty minutes. He was happy to greet the guests with help from my sisters until I got there. I took a deep breath to calm myself down. It had been a really hectic day. I had been running around all day trying to decorate the enormous hall we had hired for the occasion, until finally my friends volunteered to take over when I needed to return home in anticipation of the make-up artist. It was the evening of my engagement party, when my partner and I finally publicised our commitment to each other. We had been planning the event for over two months, having sent out all the invitations six weeks earlier. We found the perfect location, the right caterers, the music we wanted to be played throughout the evening, as well as agreeing on the ideal décor for the venue. Yet on the day everything seemed to be out of order.

Over a hundred guests were expected, including our family members, friends, friends of the family, colleagues and associates. The original plan was to keep it to half that number but as the invitations started to go out, the numbers started to go up. We had some relatives making the trip from interstate, and obviously his parents were flying over from Bangladesh for the occasion. As I sat on the chair in my room waiting for my hair to be done, I felt overwhelmed. This was not what I had in mind for my engagement. Even before I had met my partner, like every other girl, I had dreamt of an incredibly romantic proposal. I would not have had any problem with a clichéd proposal involving candle-lit dinners, or at the very least the element of surprise. The promise ring a few years ago was definitely a surprise but it wasn't a proposal. I had always hoped when the time was right and he was ready to take the next step, he would serenade me like I had dreamed. Instead, he barely called me up one day and asked if an engagement party sometime in the first half of this year would suit as he needed to let his family know in advance for them to be able to make the trip to Australia. We hadn't discussed anything of that sort previously. The next time I saw him, we sat down to work out the best time to have the party in order to make sure anyone coming from overseas had been given sufficient notice and we had enough time to plan things out. There was no romance in it. The thought of making it official didn't make my heart race faster; there was no anticipation, no exhilaration. It was as though we were doing something we eventually thought would happen, like second nature.

I decided to look somewhat traditional for the ceremony. I wore a sari but it wasn't exactly in the custom colour of Bangladeshi weddings, red. Instead, it was champagne with silver embroideries. I had matching stilettos and a purse. All the ornaments I wore complemented the sari including the gold ear rings I received as a gift from my partner's parents, and the gold chain necklace from my mother. The woman doing my hair decided to do it in a bun with small plastic flowers pinned on the one side to match my sari. When she eventually told me she was done, I stood up slowly but realised I was a nervous wreck. I was shaking. It didn't help wearing something I wasn't comfortable in and only wore a handful of times in my entire life. However, it was important to our families that we conveyed some traditional values during the ceremony, including what we wore. Therefore I was happy to oblige. I looked at my reflection in the mirror as I composed myself. Even I couldn't recognise the person staring back at me. She looked more mature, and more of a woman than she had ever done before. She had some stress lines on her forehead but hoped those would disappear once she made her way to where she needed to be right then. I tried to muster up a smile for her.

On the way to the reception hall, I kept thinking this isn't at all how I had pictured my special day to be. Granted it wasn't my wedding day, but I had pictured my engagement to be as special, if not more. I always knew how hectic wedding days can be with all the preparation and the pressure on the day of making sure it was just perfect. So I guess in my head I saw the day I got engaged to be more special. It should be intimate. It should make me want to fall in love with my partner all over again. It should make me never want to let him go. I was glad to be taking the first step to be tying the knot with the love of my life, but there was some discontent. I couldn't help but think about how the days leading up to today had gone. My mother-in-law-to-be had arrived from Bangladesh for the occasion along with her youngest daughter. I had met them a few years ago when I went to visit Dhaka with my mother. They were very welcoming and lovely. I felt like I could belong. I was excited at the prospect of some day being able to call his family my own. But it all seemed to change with the announcement of the engagement. I was being criticised and judged at every footstep. Even my mother was criticised for not being able to raise us right. Apparently we were given too much freedom growing up and therefore didn't know how to respect men as men should be respected. She was even accused by my mother-in-law of trying to steal his son away from her, in a random row that broke out of nowhere a few days before the engagement party. I couldn't believe that a woman who had a daughter of her own, not so much younger than me, would think or feel this way. I didn't know where all this was coming from. I just put it to the stress of the events and the fact that being so far away from his son couldn't have made things easier. She also missed out on the opportunity to really get to know me and my family, especially my mother whose kindness and generosity knew no bounds. I just wished that she hadn't misjudged us and that my partner had done a better job of dealing with the unfortunate episode.

As I got out of the car in front of the reception hall, still buried in my thoughts of the days leading up to this moment, Romana ran up to the car to greet me. She gasped when she was close enough to catch a proper glimpse through the open car door. I took her right hand as she held it out to me with mine, as I grabbed the sari with my left to make sure it didn't get caught under my feet as I tried to step out.

"You look amazing!" she exclaimed. "I couldn't tell from a distance if it was really you. Incredible!"

"Thank you sweetheart. How is everything in there?" I asked anxiously.

"Coming along okay. More than half the guests are here and seated. Mum got the caterers to start serving entrée. Bhaiya is waiting for you at the door."

"OK! Let's go!" I said taking one last deep breath.

My partner greeted me at the door with a tired smile on his face. He looked handsome in a black suit, a white shirt and a tie, but there were circles clearly visible under his eyes. I smiled back at him and then took my position next to him at the door. The guests continued to flow in. The noise at the hall grew louder as everyone started to mingle. A friend of my partner's took charge of the music with supervision from Romana on the sequence of songs. The music soon blasted from the speakers. After almost every seat seemed to have been occupied, I excused myself to be able to say a quick hello to my colleagues before having to run up to take mine. Everyone commented on how much they loved my look. I thanked them gracefully, and then joined my partner on the stage. I had decorated the stage myself early that morning. We were surrounded by marigolds and roses, in true Bengali tradition. I had added some beautiful candles as well, but put them inside lanterns, to establish a more demure ambience. Sumara soon came up onto the stage, took the microphone and started off the evening's proceedings. Once all the formalities were out of the way, we exchanged the engagement rings. Our parents gave us their blessing. Then our closest friends made their way onto the stage to congratulate us.

The caterers started to serve the main course almost on cue. It was an infusion of Bangladeshi dishes with more western items. There was enough variety to keep everyone happy, whether they were vegetarian or meat-lovers. The chatter grew quieter as everyone began to dig into the food. My partner and I walked around, mingling for about fifteen minutes, before we took our seats at the table next to the stage. We were hungry and determined to devour what the caterers had ready for us. Once I started to eat though, I soon felt full. So instead I turned to Nilie, Ashleigh and Jema, who were sitting at the table next to me on the left.

"It must be the nerves. I don't feel so hungry anymore. Are you enjoying the meal?" I enquired.

Jema was the first to answer. "Of course! Everything is delicious!"

"Thank you so much girls for helping me out with finishing the decoration of the hall. It looks beautiful. I couldn't have done it without you."

"Not a problem. I am glad you like it," Nilie responded with a smile.

Turning to my partner who was sitting on my right, I added, "And thank you so much for greeting the guests when I was running late."

"No drama," he said patting my thigh under the table.

"It is the most normal thing on the planet for the girl to be running late to her own engagement party," Nilie paused, then continued, "Or wedding or birthday. Anything really."

Ashleigh finally got her head out of the plate and said, "For you, Nilie, yes of course 'at anything.'"

We all laughed at how true her observation was, except for Nilie of course, who just stuck out her tongue. Romana came around to check if we were all being well looked after. I replied that I was waiting for the dessert to be served like I normally did. She let me know it was on the way but we needed to cut our four-tiered chocolate cake first before the caterers were allowed to bring out the desserts. My partner and I excused ourselves from the table and headed towards where the cake was now strategically placed in the centre of the dance floor. As we took our position behind the cake, all eyes looked up at us. We cut the cake, smiled for the cameras and went back to our seats. As soon as I saw the traditional sweets like *roshmalai*, *shondesh*, *jilapi* and *gulab jamun* being brought out from the kitchen, my stomach began to grumble. My partner looked towards it and said, "Patience, little one". I smiled at him. His eyes looked greedy as well. Normally he wasn't as much into sweets as I was but after the day we have both had, I was sure he would eat anything that was put onto a plate for him.

Twenty minutes after the sweets had been served, Romana walked up onto the stage, took the microphone and requested the guests to join her on the dance floor. It didn't need anyone much convincing. All my friends as well as Romana's went up onto the dance floor. Sumara came up to my partner to say he should take me and join the guests as well. He asked me to accompany him, so I danced with him for a little bit. However, I soon found it rather difficult to be dancing in a sari, so I had to head back to the table. I sat next to my mother and watched my partner take centre stage. He danced up a storm. Romana and her friends even performed a pre-rehearsed dance routine to entertain the guests. Even Sumara, who I had never seen dancing, took to the floor. Whenever I felt tempted, I walked back to join them and returned back to my seat when the sari got out of control. It was fun watching the crowd though when I would be sitting down, glad to have all the eyes in the room away from me for a change. The night had been somewhat nerve-wrecking so I was delighted to see that everyone present was enjoying themselves.

As it neared midnight, the guests started to say their goodbyes. Soon after, the hall was nearly empty. Sumara began to gather the equipments to start cleaning up, soon joined by Ashleigh and Jema. Nilie helped Romana get all the presents we had gotten from the guests into the car. My mother assisted the caterers in the kitchen so they could wrap up and leave. Once everyone except our family members had left, I gave Sumara a hand with the clean-up after saying goodbye to Ashleigh, Jema and Nilie. We needed to leave the venue exactly as we found it when he had hired it. My partner said he would drive his parents back to his apartment, and then join me later to help out. I said goodbye to his parents, adding that I would join them for breakfast the following morning. He left with them in his car. By then both my mother and Romana had lent us their hands with tidying up the hall. Twenty-five minutes after he had left, we had reorganised the hall as we were meant to. I was almost ready to leave the venue when my partner called.

"I was calling to see if it was okay if I didn't come back to the hall," he said over the phone.

"We are almost done with the cleaning up, so you don't have to help out anymore." I advised him.

"Great. So I will just see you tomorrow then?" he asked.

"I could come over on the way to the house to see you for five minutes." I suggested. I wanted to kiss him goodnight. After all, we did just get engaged. I would have preferred to be with him for longer, but it wasn't going to be possible given his parents were staying with him at his tiny apartment. They were exhausted, I was sure.

"Don't worry about it. I am pretty tired myself, so I am about to hit the sack. See you in the morning. Good night."

"Good night." I replied in a sad tone before hanging up.

Perfect. All alone without my partner on the night I get engaged, I thought to myself. All I wanted to do was share the experience with him after such an eventful day, especially when the event was significant for the both of us. Feeling disappointed, I followed my family out of the hall as my mother locked up. Romana joined me in my car, whereas Sumara took mum in the other.

I couldn't help but blurt out to Romana "What an anti-climax!", as matter-of-factly, referring to how the day had ended, when I started up the engine. I felt completely drained as I finally rested my back against the seat of the car.

Chapter 21

Six months had passed since the engagement when genuine doubts about marrying the love of my life started to surface. Regardless of the sheer effort it took us to get ourselves back on track the last time he raised his hand at me, the same occurred again. The only reason I was convinced to go through with the engagement, apart from the fact that I was still madly in love with him, was because he swore on his mother's life he would not do to me what his father did to his mother. When I asked him one day why he was angrier at his father than his mother on how his family had drifted apart, he had responded that abuse was part of the reason. He never could forgive his father for it. The only difference was that his father raised his hand on his mother only once during their marriage of three decades, for which his son could not forgive him. Yet the same son had re-enacted the act over and over again on his fiancée. The length of time his parents had been married did not excuse the act but it was his hypocrisy I could not bear. He repeated it again just six months after the engagement, during another trivial power-play episode staged by him. This time my confidence in the relationship was truly shattered.

This time I was sure I couldn't have faith in his word. He got on his knees once again and begged for forgiveness when it happened, but the difference was that to me this time it seemed more like a ritual than the truth. I knew I was a fool to believe him the times before when I did. If he could do so even after we were engaged, there was no guarantee it won't be a regular occurrence once we were married. I needed to get away, take some time to think. I knew what decision I would eventually have to make but I didn't know how to bring myself to do it. When I was around him, I was constantly thinking about how he made me feel. It made me confused. When I was with my family I thought about how ashamed they might feel if I called off the engagement. When I was alone, I felt even worse. I needed time to work through what it is that I wanted for myself before I could relay my thoughts to anyone I cared about or those who cared about me. I was standing at the biggest cross-roads of my life: *do I knowingly continue on this path sacrificing my happiness for the name of love or do I learn to stand up for myself in order to break free from a possible life of endless misery?*

I thought about how scared I was at times of feeling lonely. I often remembered of the time as a child when I thought my family had left me and how frightened I felt all alone. I must have been barely six years old. My father was at work and my mother had to take my younger sister to the doctor while my older sister was at her friend's. I was promised my mother would return within an hour, so I kept busy with my toys. I didn't want to say goodbye to my mother and younger sister at the door, but I put on a brave face, saying I would be alright. As soon as I heard their footsteps die, I brought the radio-clock and put it beside me on the floor where I was playing with my dolls. I kept looking at it every five minutes, counting down till the hour was over. It felt like forever, but finally an hour had passed. My mother, however, had not returned with my sister. I gave it another five minutes, then another five. Eventually it had been seventy-five minutes, but no sign of my family. We didn't have mobile phones in those days and we couldn't afford to have a home phone either. There was no one I could call. Slowly tears started to stream down my face as I thought I had been abandoned. I couldn't control it much longer. It soon turned into a shrieking fit. I started to bang on the door with both hands as I couldn't open it to get out and have a look around. I screamed my heart out and cried for my mother. I kept shouting out, *"Ammu, please come back! Please come back, Ammu! You can't leave me here on my own. I can't live without my family. God, please bring them back, god. Please bring them back!"* Finally when I heard the key turn in the hole and saw my mother enter through that door, I jumped up and put my arms around her. I held her tight. She asked if I as okay and I simply said that now I was.

This time the person I trusted the most had broken my trust. Now the only person I trusted was I. I had to find a way to get away from him without him realising what was going through my head. If he knew what I was thinking, I was sure he would try to convince me otherwise. He would tell me everything would be alright once we were married. He would blame the current situation on the pressures of having to balance this relationship, his family, studies and work. He would blame the stress on finances and his inability to build the life right now that he eventually wanted for us. He would ask for my help, only to feel down in the dumps soon after, for having to ask it. I knew I really could not take that chance. He tended to scrutinise himself for not being the best provider, then when he had reached his lowest point, blame all his failures on me. He was as amazing at building me up as he was at breaking me down.

I had completed my university degree that year. After graduation, I had long two-months off before I needed to join the workforce. This was the perfect opportunity. He knew how much I enjoyed travelling. So if I told him I wanted to go for one last trip before having to commit to full-time work, I hoped he would be supportive of it. Therefore, one evening, I asked him to meet with me in the nearby park close to our homes. I met him at the entrance and we walked together towards the lake. As we walked by the lake, and fed the ducks bread crumbs, we started discussing our plans for the next few months. He had to take summer classes to make up credits for some of the subjects he had failed earlier in the year. I was going to be all alone at home without work or studies.

"I was thinking", I started to say gathering up courage, "What do you think about me making the most of the last university break I have before I started working full-time?"

"How long do you have off?" he asked.

"A little over two months."

"You can take up some sort of a short course to keep yourself occupied if you like."

"I kind of had something else in mind." I interjected.

"Hmm . . . What did you have in mind?"

"You know how much I love travelling . . ."

He cut me off. "You are not thinking of taking another trip now, are you?"

"I was really hoping I could do some volunteer work in Africa. I had always thought about it while at university, but it never happened. This was the perfect time to do it. Don't you think?"

"No way I want you to go to Africa! Who would you go with?"

"I don't know. I am sure I can find group trips if I look online."

"No, baby. I am really not comfortable with this."

"I really wanted to do this. I need to feel like I have made some difference in someone's life."

"You have made a difference in mine. Is that not enough?"

I couldn't tell if he was being sarcastic or genuine.

"Oh, come on! You know what I mean." I responded.

"No, I am not sure this is such a good idea. Besides, it is not exactly the safest place in the world to travel on your own."

"We have lived in Bangladesh." I said giving me a sardonic smile. "You know things get exaggerated on the news. It will be fine."

"No, I am not comfortable with you going to Africa."

"Baby, I really was hoping you will be supportive of this."

"I am sorry, I can't." He paused for a moment, thinking. "However, if you wanted to go and visit your relatives in the US, I would be ok with that."

"It is always nice to see them, but that's not exactly what I was hoping to do this summer." I replied sounding a little disappointed.

"If you are going to leave me again even though you promised you wouldn't, this is the best I can suggest."

I stared blankly at the water for a few minutes. I rationalised with myself—what I needed was distance from him to help me make the most important decision of my life. Given the situation, I didn't think I could waste this opportunity. When I opened my mouth again, I had a more optimistic tone.

"I guess that's a compromise. It would be really nice to see all my cousins. It *has* been four years already since I have seen them last."

"You can go for a couple of weeks to the States. I am sure they will be happy to see you as well, as an engaged woman."

Two weeks would be nowhere near enough to help me answer the question I was considering. I couldn't return without a sure-fire response.

"I have a whole two months off, so I was hoping to make the most of it. Once I start full time work, when will I ever get so much time off at once? I was hoping may be six weeks?" I suggested.

"Oh wow! That's such a long time." He paused to think before continuing. "Well, would a month be a nice compromise?"

"I guess." I replied in an incredibly mellow voice, but I was pleased with the outcome.

We sealed the deal with a kiss. As soon as I got back home that evening, I searched for flights on the internet. The sooner I booked the flights, the better. It meant he would be unable to change his mind. I didn't want to give him an opportunity to change his mind. I was desperate to get away without raising any alarm bells. I wanted absolutely no one to influence my decision. If the decision I came back with was to stay and continue my life with him, maybe I would tell him the truth one day. There was one thing I was certain of though—today was not going to be that day.

After carefully searching the web for over an hour, I found some reasonably priced airline tickets. Rather than booking them straight away, I looked for a little while longer, when I discovered some deals where I could pay only slightly more to include a stop-over in London via Bangkok, Kuala Lumpur or Singapore. I decided it would be lovely to see my aunt who was residing in London at the time, before making my way to New York. In the US, I intended to visit at least half the cities where I had relatives. My options were New York, Los Angeles, Dallas, San Antonio, Phoenix, and Chicago, amongst others. I was searching for flights which would take me to New York via London, and let me leave the States via Los Angeles. While in the States, I could buy cheap domestic flights and move around as I pleased. The more I spent time planning out my trip, the more I realised this is exactly what I needed. Visiting my relatives would assist me with getting back to my roots and re-inventing the family values I was brought up with while living in Bangladesh. On the other hand, the days I would spend on my own along the way, including the stop-over in Asia, would help me sort out my feelings solo. I knew I wasn't going to discuss the doubts in my head concerning my relationship with my relatives. Even so, observing my aunts and uncles, or my married cousins would help me realise what it is that I wanted—for now, and for the longer term.

By now I had become an expert at finding well-priced tickets covering multiple destinations that didn't break my bank. Besides, I didn't have to pay for accommodation while I was staying with the relatives. I had also worked incredibly hard earlier in the year and saved up all throughout. Therefore, even though I was technically still living the life of a student, I was able to afford this trip without giving it a second thought. Travelling was my hobby, so I sort of had a reserved fund for that purpose, even though the last time I had been overseas was when I had just met my partner for the first time. Since then we had travelled a little around Australia. I was unable to convince him to travel any further. He was a complacent type of a person, so he preferred spending his holidays leisurely at home. I, on the other hand, loved to go out there and see all that there was to see. When I returned from my last trip, he made me promise him I would never travel without him ever again. He also promised to make my dream of exploring Europe possible, with him, during our honeymoon. As we got closer to our wedding, that dream seemed to be getting further away.

When we had started dating seriously, we were sure by the time we were ready to get married, both of us would be working. We would have saved up enough to buy a house together, and travel to Europe for our honeymoon. However, since being engaged the realisation hit that it wasn't the reality. It didn't matter to me that we couldn't afford to buy a house together right now or go to Europe for our honeymoon. Those were all materialistic things I could easily forego if he made me happy. I was a little upset that he didn't put more effort into completing what he had set his mind to do—complete his bachelor's degree. He was smart but purely lazy. Neither did he track well for the completion of the course, nor did he make the decision to let go in order to be able to move forward with an apprenticeship of some sort. I would have been supportive either way. He, on the other hand, didn't seem to care. He took everything for granted. In all honesty, absolutely none of these mattered to me as much as the fact that he made me feel miserable by the sheer power of how he treated me. He broke me down completely with constant criticism, verbal and physical abuse. I was not the confident girl anymore that I once was. I would always second-guess myself, or be downright scared of getting hurt. I lived in fear.

Once I had the itinerary sorted, I contacted my relatives to let them know which dates I would be travelling. Everyone was extremely excited to hear the news of me gracing them with my presence. I felt loved and cared for. Every day that got me closer to the trip, I was more and more upbeat. I was not only looking forward to the visits, but also to finding the ultimate answer to my quest. At that point, little did I know that it would take me several more months after my return to finally execute the last chapter of the treacherous saga that was my relationship.

Chapter 22

I woke up with a big grin on my face.

"It's Friday!" I whispered cheerfully as I jumped out of bed. I loved Fridays at work: casual-wear, no important meetings, long lunches, multiple coffee-breaks, finishing early unless something urgent came up at the last minute, and the ultimate way to end the day—hanging out afterwards with all my favourite colleagues until the early hours of Saturday morning. The Friday night shenanigans had become a ritual over the past five months where all the new graduates from our company, any other fun colleagues from our respective teams or friends who were graduates at competing firms, gathered to end another week of hard-work with a bang. I had been taking part in it since my break-up three months ago. Initially it was a way for me to keep myself occupied, and meet people who weren't a part of the life I had before with my ex-fiancé. Over time it grew into much more than just that. I strongly bonded with most and my relationship with each grew stronger. I didn't just consider them 'colleagues' anymore—they were my friends.

Even though these Friday nights were a regular occurrence, a ritual to which we were the pilgrims, we had all started to hang out beyond that. It had spilled to house-parties, day-trips, long-drives, weekend shopping, dinners and more. Those within the group with partners had taken the initiative to introduce their better halves to the rest of us. It was a gesture that unmistakeably suggested willingness to really be in each other's lives as friends and not just as people you see in the office. When anyone's birthday came around, we were all invited alongside the long-term friends. The network started to grow bigger and stronger. I had of course invited Jema, Ashleigh and Nilie to many of these events when I eventually felt ready to be able to merge my life before and after the break-up, without allowing the past to impact my present.

The past three months had been a heave of ups and downs. Some days I felt like I was totally over my ex-partner and other days I was engulfed into deep depression of loneliness. Yet not once did I feel regret at finally doing what I knew I should have done a long time ago. As the weeks passed by, I realised the break-up on my behalf was an act of kindness not just to myself but to him as well. I hoped he would stop pretending that everyone who cared about him would hang around no matter what he did. I wished with all my heart that it would eventually help him realise not to take loved ones for granted; that his actions had consequences; and that he needed to start putting in more effort into his life rather than just let it pass him by. I hoped he would grow to be a better man and make some woman really happy some day. As much as I had dreamt of that girl being me, since I made the decision to call off the engagement I realised that it wasn't meant to be. Our relationship was just another journey to help us find what we were both eventually looking for.

I woke up this morning feeling optimistic. I was ready to let go of the past, in order to help me truly move forward with the future. I realised it might take me some time to heal completely. I knew I wouldn't be able to let anyone in as easily as I had let him in. The damage that had been caused would take a while to be fully repaired. However, I woke up feeling optimistic because I realised that I had finally let go of the anger I was holding onto. It was a huge leap for me, and I was looking forward to celebrating it with all my new-found friends later that day. I put on a colourful dress, a mesh of pink and purple, which reflected my mood accurately. My matching make-up was just enough to look professional while at the same time convey the message that I had plans for the evening. My hair was neatly straightened. My high heels were trendy and fashionable. I finished off my look with a pair of earrings, the only jewellery I had worn except for my watch, which screamed, "*I may be at work but it's Friday!*" As I headed out the door, I let the cool fresh breeze embrace my face. I inhaled the autumn air with a sense of purpose, and marched onto the street.

The day passed by incredibly quickly. I arrived at the office around eight-thirty in the morning. I worked on a document for a little while that needed to be reviewed. As soon as the clock hit ten, I joined a couple of the colleagues from my team to head downstairs for coffee. We went into my favourite coffee shop in the food court and talked about plans for the weekend over cups of freshly brewed café latte. When I came back to my desk half an hour later, I found an email from one of my graduate friends, Sonria, sent to about ten of us asking if we wanted to meet at the foyer at twelve-fifteen, to walk together to the lunch which had been locked into our Calendars for several weeks. One of the graduates was celebrating his birthday and he had sent out an invitation two weeks ago to join him for lunch. I replied to the email saying 'Yes!', then attended to the other emails in the inbox awaiting my response. Before I realised it, it was twelve-fifteen when Sonria 'pinged' me on our internal instant messenger service to let me know she was heading downstairs. I locked my computer, grabbed my handbag and rushed out.

Seventeen people had gathered in the foyer, including Matt, the birthday boy. I kissed Matt on the cheek and wished him a happy birthday. Ten minutes later we were all strolling down Flinders Lane to Terra Rossa, well-known amongst us for its superb Mediterranean cuisine. It was a leisurely lunch as most lunches on Fridays happened to be, if we didn't have a deadline to meet. Especially when there were birthdays or team lunches involved, sometimes it tended to stretch to as long as two hours. That was exactly what happened this afternoon. We talked about work, shenanigans of the Friday before, plans for that evening, each of our plans for the weekend as well as a lot of harmless teasing—a norm at any of these gatherings. There didn't need to be a reason or a purpose, we all loved to pull each other's legs as if we were still in high-school. After lunch we all dispersed in different directions depending on who worked in which office building for the company. Those that worked in the same building as I walked with me. When I finally got into the elevator to take me to my floor, Matt asked if I would be ready to leave work around four or four-thirty. I said that I should be able to and would email others to let them know about the meeting time.

I tried to focus on getting back to the document I had started reviewing that morning, but found it quite difficult. There was constant interruption from various colleagues at different times who found Friday afternoons at work painful to bear. I sometimes welcomed the interruption but had to turn down an offer to go and grab some yogurt around four. I had half an hour to wrap things up before I could call it a day. I was extremely exuberant when I finally shouted "*Have a great weekend everyone!*" and walked out of the floor to join others at the meeting point. The usual Friday crowd had started to gather in the foyer as the chatter picked up while we stood around in a circle. Everyone who was ready to leave work early had gathered between four-thirty and five. The others sent text messages or called to say they would meet us at the venue when they were done. Finally at five in the afternoon, our large crowd started to move towards Federation Square. Destination: Riverland. Riverland was a bar on the banks of the Yarra that over time grew to be a regular venue for our Friday night drinks whenever the weather was pleasant. Of course it was definitely more often frequented during summer.

As the evening wore on, the crowd grew thicker. Some left the scene for an hour or so to grab dumplings for dinner before returning to continue on with the night stronger than before. Those with partners waiting for them at home left around eight or nine in the evening to be able to catch the earlier trains back. Anyone willing to continue stayed on, and a group of us changed venues around eleven to a nearby bar with a dance floor and louder music. Finally at about one in the morning I announced that I was leaving in order to be able to catch the last train home. A smaller group, consisting of those who wanted to catch the last train like I, joined to walk with me to Flinders Street Station. At the station I said goodbye to everyone at the platform and jumped on the Craigieburn line. Habitually I took my mobile out of the handbag and checked to see if there were any messages or missed calls. What I saw was not something I would have expected in my wildest imagination. Yes, there was a text message waiting for me alright. It read:

"Hi. How are you? Are you still mad at me? I think we need to talk. Can I come over?"

It wasn't so much the words that shook me; it was the sender—my ex-fiancé. I stared at the text for at least ten minutes to get my head around it. Finally when I regained my composure, I wrote a message to one of the guys I was hanging out with earlier that evening, to get some friendly advice on how to respond to this. I needed a man's opinion on what to make of it. I wrote:

"I just received a text message from my ex, completely out of the blue. He sounds as though he thinks we are still together but just mad at each other or something, and wants to come over. What should I do?"

I hit the 'send' button. Not even a minute later my mobile started to ring. I picked up without thinking to look at the caller ID. An angry voice blasted at me from the other end.

"Ex-fiancé? Your *ex-fiancé*? Who did you intend to send that message to? Is it another boy? Are you seeing someone?"

Completely flabbergasted, I started to stammer, "Sorry, I didn't realise I sent the message to you. It was meant for a friend."

"Who is this friend? And what did you mean by ex-fiancé?" He was still fuming, demanding answers in a raised voice.

"Look, I am on the train heading home. I can't exactly talk to you about this right now."

"Fine, then. I am coming over in an hour." He hung up without even giving me a chance to reply.

Ten minutes after I got home, there was a loud knock on the door. My first instinct was to ignore it, but

I decided to face my demons. My heart started to flutter, my throat felt dry and my stomach was doing somersaults. As I opened the front door, there was a tall, excruciatingly thin boy standing there wearing track-suit pants, a light sweater and a hat. His face was unshaven, his eyes had black circles around them and his breath smelled of cigarettes. He barged in and sat down on the single couch next to the doorway without waiting to be invited in. I shut the door behind him, and took a deep breath as he started to ramble.

"So what, we are over just like that? I wanted to wait to give you time to cool down. I was waiting for you to come to me. This whole time I thought we are on a break, we have been broken up? My parents told me you had left me, I didn't believe them. I told them, *'No, she wouldn't. She wouldn't. She would never leave me.'* They asked me to move on, but I didn't. I was waiting. Now you call me your *ex-fiancé*? What the fuck is going on?"

I had heard enough. When I opened my mouth, my voice was stubborn as my heart felt.

"First of all, you waited three months . . . **three** months to discuss this? Three months? Who does that? You just waited for me to make the first move? That's your first mistake. You never take matters into your own hands, and you procrastinate—about everything! Even with something as important as your marriage. Second, you always assumed I would never leave you. You took me for granted. All this time you took me for granted and treated me as you pleased because you assumed

I would never have the guts to leave you. Well, guess you assumed wrong. Third, of course your parents encouraged you to move on. No one else would have been happier to hear us split up than them. Instead of advising you to talk to me sooner, they advised you to move on. You know what? I am glad they did. If they had managed to knock some sense into you and got you to come to see me, maybe I would have forgiven you, and we would be married, and I would be living a life of hell. So thank goodness things turned out as they did!"

I lashed back without stopping for breath.

"So what are you saying, you are over me?"

"As far as I am concerned we had broken up three months ago. I can't go through that whole process all over again."

There was more that I wanted to add, but it remained a thought in my head.

If this was before, your sad state would have grabbed me and I would have felt sorry for you. I would have taken you back. But that doesn't work on me anymore. I can't even stand to be near you with that awful smell of cigarettes. Trying to suggest I have driven you to smoke again, to make me feel sorry for you . . . it's disgusting. I prayed every night for the strength to be able to make the right decision until one day I just woke up and knew what I had to do. I prayed every night since then to help me stay strong. I feel it in my heart I haven't made a mistake by letting you go. Nothing can change my mind now!

Gritting his teeth like a mad man, he stormed out just as he had stormed in. The loud thud of the door echoed in my ears longer than in reality. A few days later I received an email from him saying he had boxed up all the belongings I had left in his apartment, ready to be picked up. The day I picked up the box was the day I returned my engagement ring.